"A *Pilgrim's Progress* for the Xbox generation! That's what Chuck
Black has achieved i[...]
Bible told in a me[...]
sword fights, quests[...]
true Prince over the[...]

"Take up the sword [...] you and [...] carry it through the
pages of Chuck Black's Kingdom Series. You'll be held captive by
a creative journey through a distant world that leads to God's
Word…and a kingdom like no other."

—TIM WESEMANN
author of *Swashbuckling Faith:
Exploring for Treasure with Pirates of the Caribbean*

THE KINGDOM SERIES

BOOK 2

KINGDOM'S
HOPE

BILLINGS COUNTY PUBLIC SCHOOL
Box 307
Medora, North Dakota 58645

CHUCK BLACK

Multnomah Books

KINGDOM'S HOPE
published by Multnomah Books
© 2002, 2006 by Chuck Black

Published in association with The Steve Laube Agency, LLC
5501 North Seventh Avenue #502, Phoenix, AZ 85013
International Standard Book Number: 978-1-59052-680-4

"Discovery" music copyright © 2002 by Emily Elizabeth Black;
lyrics copyright © 2002 by Chuck Black
Interior illustrations by Marcella Johnson
Interior design and typeset by Katherine Lloyd. The DESK

Unless otherwise indicated, Scripture quotations are from:
The Holy Bible, New King James Version
© 1984 by Thomas Nelson, Inc.

Published in the United States by WaterBrook Multnomah,
an imprint of the Crown Publishing Group,
a division of Random House Inc., New York.
Printed in the United States of America

For information:
MULTNOMAH BOOKS
12265 ORACLE BOULEVARD, SUITE 200 • COLORADO SPRINGS, CO 80921
Library of Congress Cataloging-in-Publication Data
Black, Chuck.
Kingdom's hope / Chuck Black.
p. cm. -- (The kingdom series ; bk. 2)
ISBN 1-59052-680-5
I. Title.
PS3602.L264K564 2006
813'.6--dc22   2006005474

12 — 10 9 8

I dedicate this book to my future grandchildren.
Your place in my arms is waiting.

CONTENTS

Prologue: TREK OF DELIVERANCE 9

Chapter 1: A CALL FOR FREEDOM 11

Chapter 2: HARDENED HEART 24

Chapter 3: BROKEN CHAINS 30

Chapter 4: EXODUS 34

Chapter 5: THE CODE 43

Chapter 6: CAMELOT YEARS 55

Chapter 7: KERGON AND THE KESSONS 68

Chapter 8: KERGON'S CAPTIVES 86

Chapter 9: INTO THE JAWS OF DRAGAMOTH 93

Chapter 10: THE REGATHERING 106

Chapter 11: THE PROMISE 110

Chapter 12: A FUTURE HOPE 123

Epilogue: OF BATTLE AND OF PEACE 137

Discussion Questions 139

Answers to Discussion Questions 145

"Discovery": written for *Kingdom's Hope* 148

Author's Commentary 151

© Chuck Black

TREK OF DELIVERANCE

 My name is Cedric…Cedric of Chessington. I am traveling with the greatest noble force ever established in the kingdom of Arrethtrae and beyond. We are on a crusade of deliverance, for the kingdom is in the hands of an evil warrior named Lucius. He is known as the wicked Dark Knight. He and his Shadow Warriors control the land…but their days are short.

What lies ahead can be understood only if you know what lay in the past. You may have joined me before to hear the telling of a gallant knight and his quest to fulfill the mission given him by the King of Arrethtrae. It is Leinad's story that brings understanding to the battle I journey toward. I first met Leinad when I was just a boy. His tales of great adventure captivated me. It was not until I was much older that I came to realize that those grand stories of the kingdom were true indeed. It is an honor and a privileged duty to retell the saga of the valiant Sir Leinad and his faithful companion, Tess.

The final leg of my journey—with mounted men of valor and courage—affords time to reflect. Come with me back to the time of my mentor, Leinad, Knight of the King. His people were in bondage, but the King had called him to be the instrument of their call for freedom.

CHAPTER ONE

A CALL FOR FREEDOM

Leinad entered Nyland wearing the garb of a knight and mounted on a white stallion named Freedom. He stopped at the drawbridge and took in the splendor of the majestic castle Pyron Mid. The gate towers stood tall as if to proclaim it an impenetrable fortress that no army in the kingdom could ever hope to seize. If Fairos were to fall, it would be for one reason only: The King wanted it. Such was the case, and so it was that Leinad was chosen to accomplish the impossible. Unsure of the future but obedient to and confident in the King, Leinad was willing to be the King's sword. And so Leinad had prepared himself to challenge the mightiest force in the entire kingdom. In his heart he knew the King was with him.

The moments passed, and Leinad's stillness began to draw attention. Normally a visiting nobleman would cross the drawbridge and announce himself to the gate guards. Leinad waited beyond the threshold, a clear message of insult never before witnessed at Pyron Mid. The keeper of the gate called for another guard, and after a short exchange between the two, he called down to Leinad.

"Sir, state your name and your intentions. We shall herald your arrival to Lord Fairos."

Leinad paused before speaking. "My message is for Fairos only." Slaves, overseers, and guards within listening distance stopped and gazed at Leinad in growing curiosity.

"*Lord* Fairos is not expecting visitors, and he will not come dancing to your whims, sir," the guard replied. "I suggest you depart at once."

"My message is from the King, and I will wait here until Fairos hears it!"

The gatekeeper and the other guard exchanged words again, and the guard disappeared.

Time passed, and Leinad continued to wait. He suspected that Fairos was in no hurry to respond and was sending his own message by his delay. A general movement of people toward the front of the castle was evident as word of Leinad's arrival spread.

A group of slaves under the close watch of an overseer was returning to the castle with a supply of bricks. As they passed, an adolescent boy caught Leinad's eye. Leinad smiled with compassion at the young lad, whose face revealed the weariness and subjection of a slave without hope. In a moment of transformation, the lad's face brightened in hope and disbelief. He turned to the slave next to him, and Leinad could hear the excitement in his voice.

"It's Leinad!" he exclaimed.

"Leinad's dead, boy," the man retorted. "And this man's

a dead man too." The man turned to look, but the overseer shouted and cracked his whip above their heads.

Fairos finally appeared on the gate wall above Leinad with an air of authority and arrogance. Keston, the captain of the guards, and five of his men appeared in the gate below a moment later.

"Tell me, sir!" Fairos shouted. "Who is it that insults me with his presence and an absurd message from a make-believe king?"

Leinad sat tall upon Freedom. "My name is Leinad, and I come by the authority of the King and by the might of His sword. I do not wish for harm to fall upon you or any of your men. Hear the words of the King: 'Let My people go!'"

Fairos did not move or respond, but the people did. An audible rumble of voices flowed like a wave around the castle. Keston responded too. Leinad had humiliated Keston before his own men. His anger was obvious. He drew his sword and advanced with the five guards. Partway to the drawbridge, Fairos spoke.

"Hold, Keston!" He paused. "Well, you certainly are not a nobleman, but rather a slave with no name in Nyland."

"I am no slave, but I *am* a servant…a servant of the one true King and His people," Leinad said.

By now all labor had ceased, and most of the castle guards were on the wall or exiting the gate below to see the activity beyond.

"Kill him, Keston!" Fairos commanded.

Keston and the five guards resumed their advance toward the drawbridge. Leinad dismounted on the far side of the bridge and drew his sword. When Keston reached the bridge, he halted his men.

"Stay here—I will finish him myself!" he said.

Leinad walked onto the drawbridge toward the castle. Keston's gait was sharp and full of fury.

The two met near the middle of the bridge, and Keston did not break his stride or offer the greeting of mutual respect normally exchanged before such a fight.

Keston's sword struck first with intense aggressiveness. Although Leinad had seen Keston train and fight, he had learned from his father never to underestimate his opponent. He parried Keston's barrage of cuts and slices and studied him. Keston's frustration became increasingly obvious as he attacked with combination after combination against an opponent whose defense was flawless. Leinad matched Keston's speed and power while he held his ground.

"I have no quarrel with you, Keston," Leinad said. "It is Fairos I must face."

"You will only face Lord Fairos on your back after I am through with you, bleeding and dying at his feet!" Keston said in a rage. "That sword will belong to me once and for all!"

"Very well, Keston. The choice is yours."

Leinad deflected Keston's last offensive cut, and his last cut it was, for Leinad began an advance that brought gasps from the onlookers. With increasing speed and power, Leinad's sword sliced through the air faster than Keston could counter. With each break in Keston's defense, Leinad made precision cuts in his flesh. First, the tip of Leinad's sword cut through Keston's left shoulder—then his right thigh—then his abdomen. Within a moment, Keston was bleeding from a dozen places, but his sword arm was still whole. Leinad's dominance was obvious, and Keston was growing weak from exhaustion and loss of blood. His rage turned to submission and defeat.

In a last-chance effort, Keston tried to deflect a chest high cut and lunged forward with a thrust at Leinad's chest. Leinad easily parried the thrust to his left and executed a powerful bind on Keston's sword that forced it from his grip. Without a sword and bleeding from all over his body, Keston fell to his knees before Leinad with his arms open wide.

"Have mercy, Leinad," Keston pleaded. "My life is in your hands."

Just then Fairos, full of rage, broke through the crowd and started across the drawbridge.

Leinad stood before Keston with his sword pointed at Keston's chest. "As I said, Keston, I have no quarrel with you. Swear that you will raise no sword against me or the King's people, and you shall live."

"I swear—"

A sword cut through his chest from behind.

"You have disgraced me and all of Nyland!" Fairos withdrew his sword from Keston's body. "No one does this to Lord Fairos and lives!"

Keston fell to the ground and died. Leinad stepped back in horror, amazed that Fairos was capable of such ruthlessness to one of his own. Fairos raised his sword to Leinad with hatred in his eyes.

"You are a worthless slave, and I will dispense with you once and for all."

The last time Leinad had fought Fairos, he'd faced death at the edge of Fairos's sword. But that was before he met the King. This time was different, and so was Leinad. His sword belonged to the King, and so did his mission. He remained silent and prepared himself for the fight, for he knew that Fairos had shut his ears to words.

The two men engaged each other. Both were extremely skilled—both were very aware of the other's mastery. Fairos's arrogance was obvious, and he made an offensive advance as if to probe Leinad's abilities. The swords screamed through the air, steel to steel. Fairos brought a powerful slice across Leinad's torso. Leinad met the sword with the flat of his blade and countered with a quick cut across Fairos's chest. Fairos could not regain protection with his sword in time and jerked his body backward to escape the deadly edge of Leinad's blade. Seeing that Fairos was off balance, Leinad brought another slice from the right. Fairos pulled his sword across his body to meet Leinad's sword, but the force of impact was too much to counter, and the razor sharp edge of Leinad's sword cut into Fairos's left shoulder.

Fairos did not flinch from the pain, and the wound did not appear to be deep. He paused and glared at Leinad and then at the blood trickling down his arm. Leinad knew that Fairos had been victorious against many mighty enemies, but he saw something in Fairos's expression that he had never seen before—fear.

Leinad allowed Fairos his moment of reflection and was thankful for a break to regain his breath and his composure. He was strained but not exhausted. The King had not only trained him beyond mastery, but had conditioned him as well. The few times Leinad had fought outside of training, he had dealt with fear himself. Now, however, there was no fear within him. He was not fighting for his life; he was fighting for the King and for the people. He carried the mission, the sword, and the skill of the King with him.

By now the people watching from the castle and all the other onlookers were nearly still, watching two masters fight to the death. Those on the fringes of the scene were compelled to draw closer.

From the heights of the castle gate wall, Lady Fairos and her son watched with apprehension. "Kill him, Father! Kill him!" the boy screamed.

Leinad readied himself for the next engagement. "The King demands the freedom of His people," Leinad said sternly. "Release them and no one will die."

"You are a fool to believe that I would give you that which has made me great," Fairos said.

Fairos attacked with renewed fury, as a warrior fighting for his life and his reputation. The sound of the clashing swords rang out over the silence of the awestruck crowd. The fight moved from one side of the drawbridge to the other.

Leinad became more aggressive and advanced relentlessly on Fairos until he was nearly off the castle end of the drawbridge. Both men were beginning to tire, but Fairos's fight began to look desperate. He returned an aggressive combination to put Leinad in retreat. As Leinad moved back, he stumbled over Keston's body and fell backward onto the drawbridge decking. Fairos, seeing an opportunity to finish the fight, brought a two-handed cut from above his head down toward Leinad, who was lying faceup.

Leinad rolled to the side. Fairos's blade tore into the wood of the decking, just missing Leinad's shoulder.

Leinad's rolling maneuver threw him off the draw-bridge, and he was just able to stop his plunge into the moat by grabbing the edge with his left hand. He kept his grip on his sword, knowing that Fairos would be on him in an instant. He placed his sword and right hand on the deck of the drawbridge to lift himself, but Fairos slammed his foot down on the flat blade of Leinad's sword, pinning it to the deck. Leinad looked up into the sneering face of Fairos.

"Well, slave, it looks like you have failed again. I am king here. Your death will be my proclamation!"

Fairos raised his sword to deal his final blow to Leinad. In an instant, Leinad used his left elbow as leverage and pulled with all his might to yank the sword from beneath Fairos's foot. The smooth steel of the blade slid easily on the decking. Fairos's foot slid forward with the blade, and he fell backward onto the drawbridge near its edge. Leinad threw his sword on the drawbridge and swung his body away from Fairos and onto the decking. Fairos was preoc-cupied with keeping himself from falling into the moat, which allowed Leinad enough time to reach his sword.

When the scrambling was over, the two men once again faced each other.

The fight wore on, the two swords a relentless blur. The onlookers continued to assemble and position themselves for a better view.

Leinad drove the fight hard, and Fairos could only defend and retreat. The endurance of the prime of youth, the masterful training of the King, and the sword of deliverance overcame the ruthlessness of a battle experienced warrior and his arrogance. Leinad's continual barrage of powerful and precisely placed cuts eventually drove Fairos to the ground and onto his back. His sword was still in hand, but there was no more fight in him. With one final massive crosscut, Fairos's sword was blown from his grip. It skidded across the drawbridge and plunged into the murky waters of the moat below.

The mighty Lord Fairos lay helpless before his "slave." Both men were breathing hard, and sweat poured from their faces.

"I will not plead for mercy like Keston, slave," Fairos said with disgust between breaths.

Leinad stood over Fairos with the shining blade of his sword aimed at Fairos's chest. "Let the people go, Fairos," Leinad commanded.

"I will never let them go. You will have to kill me!"

Leinad looked at the guards, overseers, and slaves—all stunned, waiting for his action. He didn't want any more bloodshed. If he killed Fairos, the loyal guards could turn the scene into a massacre of the slaves. He needed Fairos to order the release of the people. It would be the only peaceful way to free them. He looked down at Fairos and stared into his eyes.

"No, Fairos, I will not kill you. I will do something far worse than that to you. I will let you live. You will live with the shame that a lowly slave on a mission from the King defeated you." He withdrew his sword and held it high in the air. He turned and faced the people.

"People of Nyland!" he shouted. "Let it be known that

by the might of the King's sword, mighty Fairos was defeated. I challenge Fairos to another contest tomorrow. If he defeats me, I will serve as a slave under his hand until my heart beats no more. If I am victorious, let this be proof that the King reigns and that He will bring judgment upon you for enslaving His people."

Leinad sheathed his sword and glared at Fairos once more. "If there is any honor left in you, meet me here tomorrow."

"I will meet you and kill you, slave!" Fairos said.

Leinad walked past him to his horse, Freedom.

TESS HAD BEEN WITH A large procession of slaves returning with a new load of bricks for the castle when she first saw the crowd gathered about the drawbridge. As the slave caravan moved closer, Tess watched the last sequence of the fight between the two men and sensed something familiar about one of them, even from a distance.

She tried to move faster, but the nearest overseer detained her. Her mind dared not think the impossible, but she could not quench the hope rising within her heart. For weeks she had mourned the death of Leinad. Then, when he spoke to the crowd, she felt as though her stomach flipped within her. She broke from the other slaves and ran toward the drawbridge despite the severe punishment she knew she would receive. The mere thought that her dearest friend might still be alive was all she needed to abandon caution and seek out the truth.

Leinad had finished speaking as she passed Barak at the head of the slave caravan.

"Leinad!" she called.

Barak released the coils of his whip and unleashed a vicious lash toward her back. "Back in line, slave!" he bellowed as the tip of his whip tore into her back.

Tess screamed and fell to the ground in pain. Barak took a couple steps forward to execute more punishment, but Leinad heard her call and her scream. He drew his sword and quickly covered the distance between them.

Barak's whip split the air again, racing to tear more flesh on Tess's back. Leinad precisely crosscut with his sword just above her head and cleanly severed one-third of Barak's whip. Leinad slowed his approach but continued toward Barak with the wrath of a protective tiger. No one around challenged or stopped him, for he had just beaten the best swordsman in all of Nyland.

Barak retreated a few steps, then pulled back what remained of his whip and directed a lash toward Leinad this time. Leinad sliced the next third off the whip. Barak threw what remained of his whip at Leinad and fell back against a cart full of bricks.

"Stop him!" Barak yelled to the other overseers, but they did not move.

Leinad closed in on Barak and pressed the tip of his sword into the fat of Barak's neck. He glared into Barak's pale white face with fire in his eyes. Barak looked like a frightened cornered rat.

"Many slaves have died at your evil hands, Barak," Leinad said. "If you ever harm another slave, I will hunt you down and bring justice by the edge of my sword. I swear it!"

Leinad turned back to Tess. She was already on her feet

and running to him. She leapt and hugged him with both arms locked around his neck.

"Hello, Sunshine," he said, gently returning her embrace.

"I thought you were dead," she said tearfully, still clinging to his neck.

"So did I. But the King brought me back."

She stepped back and looked into his face as if to reassure herself that he was real.

"Let's get out of here, Tess," he said, and they walked to Freedom.

Just before they mounted, Leinad saw Fairos walk over to Keston's body, pick up his sword, and return to the castle. The humiliation he had just experienced seemed to fuel his anger with every step. When he reached his guards across the drawbridge, he stopped and pointed to one of them.

"You! Draw your sword!"

The guard hesitantly drew his sword, and Fairos attacked him. The guard defended himself as best he could, but Fairos quickly ran him through, and he fell dead at Fairos's feet. Fairos pointed to another.

"Draw your sword!" he commanded.

Again, another fell. Then another, until all of his guards cowered before him. He threw Keston's sword to the ground and pointed toward Leinad.

"I am Lord Fairos! Tomorrow he dies! Double the work shifts of all slaves!" Fairos turned and entered the gates of his castle.

Leinad mounted Freedom and pulled Tess onto the

horse behind him. "Have faith, people!" he called. "The King will set you free. Have faith!"

Leinad took Tess to the sanctity of the countryside to let her taste freedom once again...at least for a day. ▨

CHAPTER TWO

HARDENED HEART

Leinad and Tess found shelter within a quiet grove of trees a few hours' ride from Pyron Mid. During the ride, they had talked about his experience in the desert and his training with the King.

Leinad dismounted near a brook that meandered through the trees. He helped Tess down from the horse and saw her flinch.

"How's that cut, Tess?" he asked.

"It'll be fine. It's just a scratch."

She shrugged, but Leinad turned her so he could see the wound more clearly. It was on her lower back on the right side. Most of the bleeding had stopped, but it looked painful.

"It's not just a scratch," Leinad said, wishing he had stopped and dressed the wound earlier. "We need to wash it and cover it. Come over to the water."

Leinad washed the dried blood and cleaned the cut.

Barak was an expert with the whip...Leinad could testify to that. Although the cut was not too deep, it was as long as the span of his hand. He was quite concerned since he knew that unattended wounds could fester and even cause death. He applied some of the sweet-smelling salve the King had given him.

"What's that?" Tess asked.

"It's an ointment made from a rare spice found across the Great Sea. It's called the Life Spice. My father once told me about it, but I'd never seen any until I met the King."

Leinad wrapped a clean cloth around Tess's waist and covered the gash.

"It feels better already. Thanks!" She grabbed Leinad's arm and looked into his eyes with a heartwarming smile. Tess kept her hair tied back, and she swept a few loose strands from her soiled face.

"I missed you, Leinad. I still can't believe you're alive."

"I missed you too, Tess. Every day my hope was that you would be all right until I returned," he said, returning the smile. Their temporary separation coupled with the possibility of never seeing each other again had caused them both to realize how important and deep their friendship had become.

Tess washed up in the cool water while Leinad built a fire and fixed some food. They enjoyed their meal together and talked at length about the King and their future.

"Well, Leinad, here we are again...the two of us with the whole kingdom to explore." Leinad read concern on her face. She looked earnestly at him. "I want so badly to just leave this wretched place. I don't want to lose you again, Leinad. Please don't fight Fairos tomorrow."

"You know I have to go back, Tess. The King's people will die there unless I do. We are part of them now. Don't worry, the King will deliver all of us from the hand of Fairos."

Tess looked solemnly at the ground. "I know we must go back. I couldn't leave them either. I just wish there was a better way than to see you face Fairos again."

Leinad looked sharply at Tess. "*We* are not going back. *I* am going back, and *you* are staying here, where it is safe, until I return," Leinad said.

Tess narrowed her eyes at Leinad. "I am going with you! I will run all the way to Pyron Mid if I must."

Leinad shook his head and looked upset, but he loved her courage. "Get some sleep, Tess. We both need it."

The weariness of slavery had taken its toll on Tess, and Leinad was exhausted from the sword fights earlier that day. Tomorrow was going to be another very intense day.

THE NEXT MORNING, THEY ATE their breakfast in silence.

"You're not coming with me, Tess," Leinad finally said. "I don't know how Fairos will respond, and it might get brutal. Yesterday he demonstrated just how barbaric he can be."

"I suppose you're right," Tess said. "It's much safer to leave a helpless young girl in the wilderness all alone."

Leinad couldn't help the smirk, which turned into a smile. "You are an ornery lass and have been from the first time I met you."

Leinad and Tess made their way back to Pyron Mid and arrived just before noon. The cool morning air was quickly consumed by the sun of a cloudless day. At the castle, the entire entourage of guards, overseers, servants, and slaves were gathered around the drawbridge. Leinad and Tess dismounted.

"Promise me you will not die, Leinad," Tess whispered to him.

"I promise, Tess. The King will be my strength and my assurance."

Tess took Freedom aside, and Leinad walked through the aisle formed by the crowd leading up to the drawbridge. The slaves looked more worn than usual. Leinad tried to encourage them with a determined smile, but most of them looked weary and empty. The younger ones responded enough to fuel Leinad's drive. He walked to the middle of the drawbridge and waited.

Fairos soon appeared and approached Leinad. "As you can see, I have gathered everyone so that they may witness your death today, slave. Your futile attempt to rescue these pathetic people is over, and so is your life."

"The King demands one thing from you, Fairos," Leinad replied with authority. "He made a promise to free these people. If I die today, you can be assured that another will come who is much more powerful than I. Either way, your time is short unless you let His people go."

"I am king here," Fairos said, drawing his sword, "and I swear by the power of my sword that I will never let these slaves go!"

Leinad drew his sword and took a swordsman's stance. "Then you swear in vain."

Once again, the sound of clashing swords filled the

Nyland countryside. All eyes were fixed on the duel between castle lord and former slave. The fate of all onlookers depended on these two men and the outcome of their battle. Both men knew their opponent's strengths and weaknesses well. It was not necessary to feel out the fight. Their engagements were intense and direct.

The fight raged on—positions changed, tactics changed. Leinad focused on a seamless defense and a powerful, precise offense. Though Fairos appeared to hold nothing back, the fight turned against him once again. In spite of all his skill, experience, and rage, he could not bring Leinad down. His cuts came slower, and his parries were slightly delayed. It was all Leinad needed to open the fight to his favor, and he pressed in hard.

Leinad saw Fairos gather his strength for a counterattack and feigned an opening in his defenses. Fairos brought a combination crosscut and slice followed by a powerful thrust at Leinad's chest. Leinad quickly parried the thrust and stepped aside. Fairos stumbled forward and fell to the decking of the drawbridge. Leinad quickly covered him with his sword to prevent him from rising, but there was no fight left in Fairos.

"End this misery for everyone and let the people go, Fairos," Leinad said as rivers of sweat ran from his brow.

Fairos worked to catch his breath. "I will not yield to a slave." Fairos slapped Leinad's blade with his own and began to rise. "And I will not free my slaves."

Leinad let Fairos pass to return to the castle, and it seemed to Leinad that the castle lord strode with his chin a little lower than normal.

"I challenge Fairos to another contest tomorrow so that all may see the work of the King!" Leinad shouted for all to hear.

Fairos stopped at the far side of the drawbridge and turned to face Leinad. His face projected the hate within him. He did not respond to Leinad but turned instead to Barak.

"Barak!" he yelled loud enough for every slave to hear. "Cut all of the slaves' food rations in half!" He then turned and walked to the gate of his castle. Those he passed kept their eyes to the ground.

Though he was victorious in the sword fight, Leinad stood on the drawbridge feeling completely defeated. The moan of the slaves crushed his heart and his hope. He walked to Tess and his horse.

"Some deliverer you are, Leinad," said a man by the name of Garrin. "It looks like all you'll deliver is a bunch of dead slaves!" Garrin was a man who would compromise anything or anyone to better himself. Because of his overbearing personality, some of the slaves looked to him as a leader, and he despised Leinad's encroachment on his influence with the people.

"Leave us alone," another man said. "Because of you, we're overworked, and now we're starvin' too."

Leinad and Tess mounted Freedom and left the castle grounds to the sound of jeers and taunts.

They rode in silence. What should have been a day of celebration had become a day of oppression, and Leinad felt responsible for it all.

How many will die today because of me? he asked himself.

The horse's rhythmic bounce seemed to pound that question into his mind over and over.

CHAPTER THREE

BROKEN
CHAINS

The next morning, Leinad and Tess were back at the castle. Leinad knew his mission and steeled himself against the defiance of the slaves and of Fairos's people.

Unlike the previous day, the people were not gathered around the drawbridge. They were working hard, and the oppression of the overseers was severe. Virtually the only action the slaves took that did not bring a scourging from the overseers was when they cursed Leinad as he rode by. Hungry, exhausted, and beaten, they were a people in the depths of despair and hopelessness like they had never felt before.

It was almost too much for Leinad to continue, but he saw the face of the boy who had first recognized him when he returned three days ago and found all the encouragement he needed. The boy looked up from his burden and smiled at Leinad. It was a smile that gently said, "Take us away from here." Leinad found affirmation in the heart of one boy.

Leinad took his position in the middle of the draw-bridge. There was no announcement, no herald. All knew he was there, but Fairos did not show.

By midafternoon, Leinad was still waiting in silence. He knew that Fairos could not ignore him forever. With every passing moment, Fairos was admitting defeat.

Eventually Fairos left the safety of his chamber and exited the castle gate. He rushed upon Leinad without any exchange of words.

The initial ferocity of Fairos's attack set Leinad in early retreat, and it took him some time to recover and counter with an advance of his own. But soon Leinad was aware of an attitude in Fairos's fight that he had never seen before. Though the strength of the fight was still available to Fairos, Leinad could feel his resignation to defeat. He guarded himself against a possible ruse Fairos might have planned.

The work on the castle grounds stopped once word of the fight spread. The slaves were not sure who they wished to win, for they could not imagine bearing the next hard-ship that was sure to come if Leinad was victorious again.

The fight continued and positions were exchanged many times until Leinad's back was to the castle. Fairos advanced with a quick and powerful combination just as Leinad heard the quick but quiet approach of someone behind him. Leinad knew this new attacker was close behind him, so he parried a hard thrust from Fairos slightly downward and began to sidestep and turn to face his second opponent.

"Nevin!"

The scream of Lady Fairos reached the ears of the combatants on the drawbridge, but it was too late. Fairos's young son, with his boy-size sword, had charged Leinad from behind to end his father's disgrace. As Leinad stepped clear of Fairos's deadly thrust, the boy ran full into his father's sword.

An instant of shock silenced everyone. The scream of a hysterical Lady Fairos shattered the silence. The boy looked briefly at his father and then collapsed to the deck of the drawbridge.

"No!" Fairos screamed in disbelief of the horrific scene before him. He withdrew his sword, threw it aside, and fell to the decking beside his son. He cradled him in his arms.

"My son! I've killed my son!"

Leinad stepped back in silence. Lady Fairos ran to her dead child and wept uncontrollably. Some of the castle guards approached with swords drawn, ready to do Fairos's bidding. Fairos looked up at Leinad with the face of a completely broken man.

"You have taken my honor…you have taken my son. Take these wretched people and leave me forever!"

Fairos lifted the limp body of his son and carried him into the castle. Lady Fairos's servants all but carried her back to the castle.

Leinad was shaken by the tragedy as well, but he reminded himself of the countless people that had come to an early death, some of them children, because of Fairos's enslavement of the people. He steeled himself for the monumental job that lay ahead.

He spoke to one of the guards he had once trained

when he was instructing Fairos's men. "Tell the rest of the guards and the overseers of Fairos's command to release the people. There has been enough bloodshed. We do not need any more."

The guard acknowledged and began spreading the word. The people had been enslaved for so long that they were cautious and unwilling to accept their freedom.

Leinad found Tess and Quinn, and together they began to organize the people for their journey out of bondage.

CHAPTER FOUR

EXODUS

 The people quickly gathered food and their meager belongings and prepared to leave Pyron Mid. The slave dwellings became an instant bed of frenzied activity. Anxiety, excitement, and apprehension prevailed among most of the people. They felt anxiety because they could not believe that Fairos would release them without some reason to further his own power. They were excited because never before had they been so close to freedom. They were apprehensive because they did not know where to go or what lay ahead of them. Some of the people left on their own, to return to their homelands, but most of the people were from the Valley of Nan or without a homeland altogether and had no homes to return to.

"Leinad!" Quinn called. "We're almost ready. There are thousands of people! Where do we take them? How will we feed them?"

Leinad smiled at Quinn. "Where the King's will lies, there lies the way."

Leinad and Tess rode on Freedom to the front of the mass of people. Leinad gave the reins to Tess and dismounted. He drew his sword and held it high for all to see.

"Through the King, we have been delivered," he shouted. "Let us set our hearts to serve Him as we set our feet toward freedom!"

He motioned forward with the sword and led the people northeast toward the majestic Red Canyon. Leinad glanced back toward Pyron Mid to see if Fairos pursued them, but such was not the case. He wondered how long it would take for Fairos's grief to transform to enraged vengeance.

Their journey was slow. Almost everyone traveled on foot. The few exceptions were the older people, who did not have the endurance to maintain their moderate pace. Tess promptly gave her seat on Freedom to two older women.

Leinad hoped to reach the Red Canyon by nightfall of the next day. It was just beyond the borders of Nyland, and he would feel much better once they were outside Fairos's realm.

LATE INTO THE FOLLOWING DAY, there did not seem to be any canyon in sight. Garrin found it an opportune time to create discord among some of the people. Leinad called for Quinn to take Freedom and scout the land before them. Within in a few moments Quinn returned.

"It's amazing," he said to Leinad. "We are almost to the canyon, but the trees ahead conceal it. The canyon is vast, but the land before and after hide it quite well."

"Thank you, Quinn. We will travel along toward the east until we are safe beyond the borders of Nyland. Then we will—"

"They're coming!" came an alarm from one of the men.

"Look!" Quinn pointed to a distant dust cloud that could be produced only by horses at full gallop...many horses.

"It's Fairos!" Garrin said to the people. "He's coming to kill us all! I told you Leinad would get us killed, and now it's happening!"

Cries of alarm swept through the people.

"You brought us out here to be slaughtered!" one man shouted to Leinad. "We were better off as slaves!"

"What will we do?" shouted another.

"Quinn, go back to the canyon and find a way down," Leinad said. "We don't have much time!"

Quinn pulled hard on Freedom's reins and galloped off toward the Red Canyon.

"Quickly, everyone!" Leinad shouted. "We've got to make the canyon before they reach us!"

The people quickened their pace, but it was still far too slow for Leinad. He kept his eye on the approaching dust cloud and estimated by its size that Fairos had called his entire mounted force down on the fleeing people.

Quinn returned shortly and dismounted. "The canyon walls directly ahead are far too steep," he said. "Off to the right there is a gorge that descends to the canyon floor, but it is narrow and long. Our people can pass only five or six wide. It will take too long to get them into the canyon. Besides, Leinad, what happens then?"

"Why don't we stop and fight them?" a large fellow said. "We outnumber them five to one."

"We have no weapons and they are mounted," Leinad replied. "It would be a massacre that none would survive. We don't have a choice. Quinn, lead us to the gorge's entrance. I will take Freedom to the rear and hurry the people."

"I'll go with you," Tess said.

"No, Tess. I need you to help Quinn direct the people to the gorge."

She looked disappointed but knew this was no time to argue. "Yes, Leinad."

Leinad galloped to the trailing people while Quinn and Tess altered their course toward the narrow gorge.

After what seemed like an agonizingly long time, the first few people reached the narrow gorge. Leinad rejoined Quinn and Tess to find a near riotous situation developing. The gorge was indeed narrow and caused a serious bottle-neck. The hurrying mass of panic-stricken people now found themselves motionless as a small trickle descended the narrow passageway into the canyon. Before long, people began to push, and the flow through the passage slowed even further. Pandemonium reigned.

Leinad rode Freedom into the mass of people near the gorge entrance and drew his sword. He pulled on the reins. Freedom reared and neighed loudly, which momentarily quieted the people.

"People!" Leinad shouted for all to hear. "You must not panic or we will destroy ourselves! The women and children will pass first. Go quickly, but do not push!"

The large man who earlier had suggested they fight Fairos's men had stepped aside to help others into the gorge.

"What's your name, sir?" Leinad asked him.

"I am Audric."

Audric was darker skinned than most of the people. His voice was low and his hands were large. Leinad assumed he was from a different region of Arrethtrae but had chosen to call the King's people his own. Though he seldom smiled, Audric's eyes were strong and gentle.

"Audric, I want you, Quinn, and Tess to manage the entrance into the gorge, and I will try to bring some order farther back."

Leinad did not have the luxury of asking anymore; he was commanding. The urgency of the situation forced him into leadership. It was a skill that did not come naturally for him, especially at his young age.

Soon the people were moving steadily into the narrow passageway down to the canyon floor. Leinad kept a watchful eye on Fairos and his approaching army. He knew it was going to be close—too close.

Tess stayed at the entrance with Quinn and Audric until the last of the people entered. The individual members of Fairos's army were now discernible.

"Tess, Quinn, Audric...get down the passageway. Quickly!" Leinad said.

"What about you, Leinad?" Tess asked.

"I will come shortly! Now get going!"

Once they departed, Leinad dismounted Freedom and looked toward the approaching army. "O my King, how will we survive the wrath of Fairos?" Leinad asked out loud.

Freedom pawed at the ground nervously. Leinad turned to descend the gorge, but froze at the sight before him. The hairs on his arms and neck stood straight, and fear was all he felt.

Before him, guarding the entrance to the gorge passageway, stood two massive warriors. Their silent approach shocked Leinad, but so did their massive arms and chests. Their swords were drawn, and their faces were stern. Besides their swords, each also carried a golden trumpet that gleamed in the late afternoon sun.

"Are you enemies or friends?" Leinad asked as boldly as he dared.

The warriors stared at him in silence.

"May I pass then?" Leinad asked.

Finally one of the warriors spoke. "The King will deliver you. Clear the people from the bottom of the gorge," he commanded.

Leinad nodded and glanced back once more at Fairos's approaching army. The gorge was long, and Leinad would have to hurry to clear it before Fairos reached its entrance. He turned to thank the warriors, but they were gone.

He mounted Freedom and entered the gorge. The descent was gentle enough to navigate on horseback. The deeper he went, the more ominous the narrow walls of the gorge became. Large stone spires rose on each side, and treacherous outcroppings seemed to hang above him to form an eerie stone tunnel.

He descended out of the hot, humid air of the plains above into the cool, still air of the canyon bottom. For a time, the only sound that broke the silence of the gorge was Freedom's panting.

Soon Leinad could hear the faint but growing sound of thousands of voices before him. It was brief comfort, however, because he heard the sharp commands of Fairos echo down through the walls of the passageway from behind.

The walls on each side seemed to rise forever above him. Except for the thin crack of light above, the path before him was dark. He hoped Freedom could see better than he.

At last, Leinad could see the passageway widen ahead, and sunlight began to illuminate his way. The sound of the people's voices was steadily growing louder. When he emerged into the brightness of the open canyon floor, he found the people confused and unsure of what to do. A small river flowed through the canyon floor.

"Now what, Leinad?" Garrin shouted. "Do we wait here for Fairos to kill us in the bottom of this pit?"

Leinad ignored Garrin and spoke sharply to the people. "Quickly, move up the canyon along the river! Fairos's army is coming, but the King will deliver us. Move quickly!"

The sound of an army of mounted warriors was growing with each passing moment. Fairos's men were nearly through the gorge entrance when a strange sound filled the canyon and hushed the people to silence. The blast of a trumpet reverberated from wall to wall in the narrow gorge and out into the canyon. Soon another trumpet joined the powerful, steady tone of the first, but at a slightly higher pitch. The mix of the two tones formed a resonant sound that built upon itself until it was deafening, even for the people on the open canyon floor.

Despite the trumpet blasts, the leading edge of Fairos's army continued to advance through the narrow gorge three horses abreast. Shouts of alarm rose up at the sight of Fairos's men.

Leinad drew his sword and broke from the rear of the people. He heard Tess scream his name, though barely because of the deafening trumpet sound.

Almost imperceptible at first, a low rumble grew until the ground shook beneath everyone. Leinad stopped just before the exit of the gorge. He could see two of the leading horses of Fairos's men stumble and collapse into the third horse beside them. One man was crushed against the gorge wall by the weight of the horses, and Leinad saw the panic on the faces of the other two as they scrambled to free themselves.

The ground shook more violently. Small rocks and dust fell from above the men and their mounts. The next few men in line tried to jump over the entangled bodies of horses and men before them, but the unsteady ground they landed on buckled the legs of their steeds, and they collapsed, adding to the chaos.

The trumpet blasts continued until the towering spires of stone that bordered the gorge passageway shifted and began to crumble. Stone shelves and outcroppings gave way to rain down on Fairos's army. The screams of dying men mingled with the panicked neighing of hundreds of horses.

Leinad turned quickly and rode to escape the descending destruction.

Come on, Freedom. Keep your legs steady, he thought as he raced back to the people.

By the time he reached them, the trumpets had ceased and the ground became still once again. The silence following a storm that had passed settled into the canyon along with the dust and debris.

Everyone looked to the gorge exit for the pursuing army, but there was none. The stone walls had collapsed, creating an instant grave for all of Fairos's army. None survived. Through the settling dust, Leinad saw two forms retreating down the canyon floor in the opposite direction.

"Leinad has saved us! He has freed us and delivered us from the hand of Fairos!" the crowd cheered.

"No!" Leinad shouted as he quieted the people. "I am not the one!" He looked sternly at them and then pointed back toward the gorge. "Behold the work of the King! He has both freed us and saved us. The King reigns!"

The people cheered and echoed his acclamation. "The King reigns!"

CHAPTER FIVE

THE CODE

The victory celebration over defeating Fairos was short-lived. The people's entrance into the canyon was sealed, so there was no choice but to find another way out. Tess, Quinn, and Audric were invaluable to Leinad as they helped organize and maintain some control of the people. Leinad led the people east up the canyon, but the walls were steep on both sides for as far as one could see.

After two days of traveling, the people began to murmur and complain. Food was scarce, and the canyon walls trapped the afternoon heat. Their only recourse was to stop and seek shade among the canyon walls until the blistering heat subsided. The cool nights were welcomed, but the people worried that the canyon would eventually be their grave.

"The King has saved us to abandon us in this desolate canyon. We will die here!" one man said in an evening assembly of the people.

"He's right!" Garrin said. "We are starving. There is no food…and no way out of this dreadful canyon! You have brought us to our destruction. I say we rid ourselves of Leinad and make our own way!"

"Listen!" Leinad said. "The King delivered us from slavery. He will not abandon us now! Tomorrow I will ride up the canyon to find a way out."

"How do we know you will not ride off and leave us for good?" Garrin said.

"Yes," said another man. "You are the only one with a horse strong enough to leave this massive graveyard!"

Quinn stood up and faced the people in anger. "Leinad came to us when he did not have to. Have you already forgotten? You are free because the King asked him to risk his life for you. May you be cursed for saying such things! Leinad will find a way out for us…as sure as the King reigns!"

Quinn's words seemed to satisfy them for now, but Leinad knew it was a temporary appeasement. He thanked Quinn for his words of support. He saw more leadership potential in Quinn, who had a charisma the people loved, than he felt in himself. His respect for Quinn was growing, and Leinad knew that he would have to rely upon him to help control the people.

THE NEXT MORNING LEINAD rose to find Freedom packed and Tess waiting for him, mounted on Freedom's back.

"And what do you think you're doing, Sunshine?" he asked.

"My duty, Leinad. I have to make sure you're not going to abandon us," she said with a wink and a smile.

Leinad responded with a cheerful smirk. "Yes, I suppose someone had better keep an eye on me."

He was actually thankful for her company. She was always a boost to his spirit, even when the rest of the world was trying him.

Leinad assigned Quinn and Audric to lead the people in the day's travel, then he and Tess went in search of a route of escape. They put Freedom into a trot to cover as much ground as possible and still be able to return to the people by nightfall.

The canyon seemed to stretch on forever. They found a few places that some of the stronger people could climb, but it was extremely risky, and most of the people would still be trapped in the canyon.

They pressed on. The scorching heat baked them as if they were in an oven.

They came to a point where the canyon split north to the left and east to the right. The northern branch was wide and looked easy to travel. The eastern branch, however, was narrow and foreboding. Before deciding which branch to take, Leinad and Tess stopped and found refuge in a sliver of shade while Freedom drank from the river.

Tess wiped the sweat from her brow. "This is quite the adventure you've brought us on, Leinad."

"Are you doing all right, Tess?" he asked.

Tess was growing up. Leinad felt their relationship changing. No longer was she a little sister. Her maturity and stature forced him to see her as more of a peer now. She was taller than most girls her age—only slightly shorter than Leinad himself. He respected her ever-present wisdom, but what he cherished most was her unwavering loyalty. Oftentimes this devotion kept him from giving up altogether. He was thankful that their relationship had changed, because he did not have the luxury of being vulnerable with anyone else.

What Leinad was only just beginning to see was how pretty Tess had become. Like slowly opening rose petals, Tess's gradual change hid her beauty from Leinad's heart. He was a young man with heavy responsibilities...responsibilities that he needed a fellow companion to bear. There was no time for anything more.

"I'm fine, Leinad. How are you holding up?"

© Marcella Johnson

"I am not the one to lead these people, Tess. The King used me to free them, but I know that they need someone other than me."

Tess was silent for a moment. "Right now, Leinad, you *are* the one. The King chose you, and you must lead them home...wherever that may be. Be confident in this for now."

He looked at her with great admiration. "How did a little girl like you grow up to be so wise?"

She blushed and turned away to look down the canyon.

Her expression transformed into one of wonder. Leinad followed her gaze and saw it too. High on the canyon wall, in the crux of the canyon branch, stood the form of a man. Though He was far away, His majestic form was unmistakable to Leinad.

"It is the King!" Leinad said in hushed reverence.

"The King?" asked Tess bewildered.

"Yes. Come on, Tess."

They rode Freedom to the base of the canyon wall, where the northern and eastern branch split, and looked up. The King was no longer visible, for the jagged stone walls before them blocked their view. Leinad searched for a place to scale the wall, and when he found one, they dismounted and began the arduous climb. Halfway up, they found a natural shelf large enough for both of them to rest on. They drank heavily from their water flasks.

"You…must go on," Tess said between breaths. "I am spent."

Leinad nodded. "I'll be back soon, Tess. No matter what happens, wait for me here."

Leinad reached the top of the canyon wall late in the afternoon. He lay for a while on the ground until he could catch his breath.

"Sir Leinad." The deep rich voice of the King seemed to strengthen Leinad. With great effort, he rose to a kneeling position.

"My King," he said, "my heart and my life are Yours."

The King placed His hand on Leinad's shoulder. "You are a faithful knight, Leinad. Come…eat and rest."

After he had replenished himself, Leinad said, "We are

trapped in the canyon, my Lord. The people are hungry and worried that they will die there."

The King looked sad. "The people are foolish and ungrateful, Leinad. But in spite of this, I will use them to establish My kingdom. You must teach them the ways of the Code."

Leinad was perplexed. "What is the Code, my King?"

"The Code is what gives the sword its strength."

"How is this possible?" Leinad asked.

"Because when one without the Code bears the sword, he does so only for himself…only for selfish gain. But the one who bears the sword *with* the Code does so for a higher calling…for a purpose greater than self-service. He does so for the King and for his fellow man. You did not defeat Fairos because of your sword. You defeated him because of what you believed in—Me. This is the meaning of the Code."

"How do I make the people understand the meaning of the Code, my King?" Leinad asked. "I have been with You and have seen You, but they have not. I have lived it and felt it, but they have not."

The King withdrew a rolled parchment from His robe. His royal seal was upon the scroll.

"Give them the Articles of the Code. They must live by them. If they do, I will make them into a great people." His firm voice rose in volume. "Through them I will establish a kingdom like the world has never seen."

The King's voice echoed across the canyon. All of nature seemed to stand still at its sound. Leinad saw the power of the King firsthand. He saw the mighty warriors that followed Him. He felt insignificant in the King's presence, yet chosen. And though Leinad did not understand it all, he followed faithfully. The King gave the scroll to Leinad, who received it humbly and knelt before the King.

"My heart and my life are Yours, my King. I will do Your bidding."

"Bring the people up the east canyon branch. There you will find another gorge that will lead you out. Travel south across the plains until you reach the Chessington Valley. This is the land I have chosen for them. This is the land to which the kingdom will come."

Leinad bowed. "Yes, my King."

The King nodded and left.

It took Leinad longer to descend the canyon wall than it had taken to climb it. He rejoined Tess on the ledge and gave her food and water. It was dusk so they decided to wait until morning to finish their descent. Leinad placed some rocks on the edge of the ledge to keep them from falling off during the night. It was cramped, and the night's sleep was not refreshing.

By late morning, Leinad and Tess had finished descending the canyon wall just as Quinn, Audric, and the rest of the people arrived at the canyon fork.

"Quinn, Audric…it is good to see you," said Leinad. "How did it go?"

Quinn looked frustrated. "We would have had a revolt on our hands were it not for Audric here. Garrin mysteriously tripped, hit his head, and was knocked out," he said with a wry smile.

Audric looked slightly embarrassed. "Sorry."

"Don't be sorry, Audric," Quinn said. "It was the most peace we've had on this trek."

Garrin worked his way to the front of the people and approached the four. His brow was furrowed, and he held a hand to his forehead as if he was suffering from a severe headache.

"Well? Did you see a way out of here?" he asked Leinad.

"No. But I know which way to go to find one," Leinad said. "Gather the people so I can talk to them."

Within a short time, all the people were gathered to listen.

"I know you are weary and tired of this journey," Leinad said, "but the end is near. I know of a way out of this canyon. We must persevere for a while longer."

"You said you did not see a way out. How do you know the way then?" Garrin said, loud enough for all to hear.

"I know because I have seen and talked to the King."

Some of the people looked skeptical and murmured to themselves.

"You expect us to believe that?" Garrin said. "Why have none of us seen Him? This is some elaborate story you have created to get these people to follow you."

"No!" Tess said. "I saw the King too!"

"And did you talk to Him as well?" Garrin asked.

Tess was silent.

"That's what I thought," replied Garrin smugly.

"The King was above us on this canyon wall yesterday," Leinad said. "He told me the way out. Farther down the eastern canyon branch there is an exit."

The people moaned, for this was the most rugged and treacherous route.

"He promised to guide us to the lush Chessington Valley and make us a great people if we live by the Articles of the Code." Leinad held up the scroll with the King's seal on it.

Garrin grabbed the scroll from Leinad. Audric moved toward Garrin, and some of Garrin's supporters moved forward. Leinad held out his hands to quiet the situation.

Garrin pointed at the people with the scroll. "You are fools if you believe this man. He is going to get us all killed if we continue to listen to him. I can tell you right now that the eastern branch will bring you nothing but death. Look…look up the northern branch. The route is easy and wide. The canyon walls look less steep farther down. Ignore this fool and travel with me. I will lead you out!"

Garrin threw the scroll at Leinad's chest and began motioning for the people to follow. Many shouts of affirmation rose in support of Garrin.

Leinad shouted for the people to be quiet.

"I cannot force you to follow the King," he said. "Make your choice now! Those who want to follow the King, separate yourselves from the others and come with me through the eastern canyon branch."

Leinad turned and began to walk toward the eastern branch. Tess, Quinn, and Audric immediately followed him, but the rest of the people hesitated. Then slowly many of them began to join themselves to the King's people. Over two-thirds of the people followed Leinad toward the rugged, narrow route. Garrin laughed and ridiculed them as he led the others northward.

The people parted, and those that traveled with Garrin were never seen again.

The stream that flowed down the eastern route was small but still provided ample drinking water for the people. Their progress was half of what it had been, and it was further slowed because the older people needed help over the jagged rocks and loose soil.

When the afternoon heat became unbearable again, Leinad halted the people to rest. They were weak because their food supply was gone, and the rough terrain exhausted them.

"Quinn, take Audric and see if you can spot another gorge that might lead out of the can—" Leinad stopped midsentence and his eyes widened.

Quinn turned to see what had captured Leinad's attention. "What in the—"

Not far ahead, antelope—hundreds of them—were leaping off the canyon wall onto the jagged rocks below. All of the people stared in amazement, wondering what could possibly make the antelope take such bizarre action.

"Only one thing could force an entire herd to jump to their deaths like this," Audric said. "A dragamoth."

A distant screech echoed down the canyon walls. The mere sound of it brought shudders to everyone. It surely belonged to the throat of a hideous beast.

"It was believed that all were dead by now," Audric said, "but I have heard of their existence in the Vale of the Dragons far south of here. It is strange that one would be in this region. We should be safe in the canyon."

The people waited in silence and listened, but all was quiet. After some time, Leinad led them to where the antelope had fallen. The people feasted on fresh game and rested in the cool shade of the canyon walls. It was a time of replenishing—of both body and spirit.

After their respite, Leinad stood on a large boulder so all could hear him.

"The King will lead us into a land that He has promised will be ours. He will make you into a great people, a people that will birth a kingdom, a people that He will call His own. You are special, for you are chosen! He has given us a Code to live by. You must honor the King by honoring the Code. Write it on your hearts and teach it to your children. Live by it day and night. Now, listen to the words of the Code."

Leinad broke the King's seal and opened the scroll to read it to the people.

"Honor the King with your life. Swear allegiance to Him and to Him only.

"Serve the King in truth, justice, and honor.

"Offer compassion to the weak, the destitute, the widowed, and the poor.

"Live for the King and serve others without cause for personal gain.

"Never abandon a fellow knight in battle or in peril.

"Equip, train, and prepare for battle against the forces of the Dark Knight.

"Serve the King and faint not in the day of battle.

"Use the sword not to seek selfish gain but rather to execute justice and the will of the King.

"Be merciful, loyal, courageous, faithful, and noble, but above all, be humble before the King and before men.

"Let your words always be spoken in truth."

Leinad finished reading the scroll and looked out over the people.

"The King reigns!" Quinn proclaimed.

"The King reigns!" the people echoed.

It was a moment that sealed them to the King. It was the beginning of a new era; it was the dawn of a kingdom reborn.

They set out on their journey once more, and Leinad led them through the narrow gorge and out of the canyon. Many days they journeyed south across the land until they found the fertile and lush Chessington Valley.

Here they made their home.

Here they built a city...the beloved city of Chessington.

CHAPTER SIX

CAMELOT YEARS

In the Chessington Valley, the people prospered. The land was fertile, the skies were blue, and the future was promising. A small river flowed through the valley and into the Great Sea to the south. Forested hills bordered the valley to the east and to the west. The countryside was picturesque. It took some time at first to establish a community with farms, ranches, shops, and trade centers, but within a few years, the city of Chessington was thriving and growing.

Leinad kept the people true to the Code and taught them to love and serve the King. He reminded them of how the King had delivered them out of Fairos's hand and brought them to this prosperous land.

Leinad was preoccupied with community affairs, something he had grown to dislike. At the age of twenty-two, he did not feel comfortable as leader of the people, and he came to rely heavily on Quinn, Tess, and Audric to help govern them. When time permitted, he instructed Quinn and Audric in the art of swordsmanship, which they learned quickly.

Though life for the people was good, it was not without some turmoil. Occasionally, thieves and marauders found opportunity to plunder the city and the surrounding farms. The people wanted protection, and they wanted a king.

"We know that the King is our true King, but we need a king we can see and who lives with us daily," one man said at a meeting in the city square.

"Yes," another said. "These marauders will continue to take from us until we can show them that we are strong enough to fight them. We need a king to do that!"

Shouts of affirmation rose up from the assembly. Leinad was disappointed and concerned.

"There is only one King in Arrethtrae," Leinad said. "To establish another would be blasphemous."

"Then call him a lord instead," a man replied.

"You be our lord and we will build a castle for you," another man shouted. "Give us an army of knights that will protect us forever!"

"No!" Leinad shouted. "I will not be a lord to rule over you. That is not what the King called me to do!"

"Then name another, or we will choose one ourselves."

Leinad's heart was heavy, for he knew he could not persuade the people. He called for the meeting to adjourn, then mounted Freedom and rode into the hills to find solitude and time to think. With the exception of Tess, Leinad found the towering, peaceful trees to be his preferred companions. They did not argue, complain, request, or petition him. They patiently waited for him and listened. He dismounted and let Freedom roam to find green grass to feed upon.

"The people are foolish indeed, my King," he said aloud. "They ask for a lord...what am I supposed to do?"

"Give them one," a familiar voice replied.

Leinad nearly jumped out of his skin at the sound of it. He turned around and smiled broadly. "Gabrik!" He ran and embraced his friend from long ago.

"Well. You've certainly grown up since I saw you last," Gabrik said, almost smiling.

Leinad realized that he had changed significantly since he'd last seen Gabrik. The tender edges of his youthful face had been replaced by the hard lines of a mature young man. Leinad was now at the pinnacle of his physical form.

"It is good to see you, Gabrik. Where have you been? Tell me what adventures you have lived over the past years."

"The war with the Dark Knight is fierce, Leinad," Gabrik said soberly. "His desire to rule this kingdom is great. My duty lies in that war, but I have been sent to give you a message."

"From the King?" Leinad asked.

"Yes. He knows the heart of the people. Give them a lord to rule over them."

"Who? Surely not I. I will not be a source of contention with the King."

"There is one who can rule the people," Gabrik said in a way that questioned Leinad.

"Quinn!"

"Yes. Let Quinn rule the people, but you must keep him loyal and true," Gabrik said.

"Quinn is well-suited for the task, Gabrik, but I know that this is not what the King truly desires for His people."

"You are right. This is not the King's way, but He will grant their request," Gabrik said. "Perhaps when they have a lord to rule over them, they will come to understand the perfect ways of the King."

Leinad thought for a moment and then took a deep breath. "I am relieved and grateful to give this burden to Quinn. He's a very good man. I will help him and do my best to keep him true to the King and to the Code."

Leinad and Gabrik enjoyed a few moments together before departing. Leinad called for Freedom and rode back to Chessington.

The people will be pleased, he thought, *but will it last?*

THE PEOPLE WERE INDEED PLEASED, for they loved Quinn. He possessed all the qualities of a leader. He was not a good leader; he was a great leader.

Leinad was cautiously optimistic. He had always known that Quinn's heart was good and that he desired to serve the King, but he knew that power and authority often changed a man...even a good man.

The people built a splendid palace for Quinn near the city square, and he raised an army of knights to protect Chessington from the bandits and marauders. They became known as the Knights of Chessington. Only the strongest, most honorable, and most skilled men were chosen. Quinn organized tournaments in the square to help select these gallant men, and he implored Leinad to train them with the sword.

Soon the threat of marauders was eliminated, and Chessington became known throughout the land as a city of wealth and power. It was a golden era for the people.

"QUINN HAS DONE WELL," Tess said one day as she rode beside Leinad on her horse.

Leinad smiled. "He certainly has."

Leinad and Tess's friendship had continued to grow over the years, and Tess was now a young woman of eighteen. The freckles of her youth had been replaced by a smooth, slightly tanned complexion. Her strawberry-blond hair was now darker, and she wore it long and in a single braid that hung halfway down her back. The posture that Peyton had taught her to maintain as a child was a constant companion to her form. Though her body was strong and fit, she was still a woman.

Leinad loved the time they spent together. Tess had never had the mentoring of a mother, and the softer edges of womanhood were not a natural part of her life. She was beautiful, but her beauty was somewhat masked by the roles she played as adviser, leader, and fellow warrior. Leinad saw her only as a kindred spirit. He never had the luxury or the time to explore a romantic relationship, and such a relationship with Tess would feel extremely awkward now.

"When are you going to get serious about training me with the sword?" she asked.

Leinad looked at her quizzically. "I have trained you as I have trained the others. You're quite good too...better than any other ladies I know of."

"There *are* no other ladies that sword fight, and you know it."

Leinad smiled. "I suppose you're right. So what's your point?"

"I want to become better than any men you know of. I want to become a master like you."

Leinad stopped his horse and studied Tess's face to see if there was any jest in her countenance. He found none. Leinad so enjoyed Tess because she never quit surprising him.

"Are you serious, Sunshine?" he asked.

She looked straight into his eyes. "As serious as a dragamoth."

"Yes, I believe you are. We shall begin training you seriously right now."

And so beginning that very day and for many days that followed, Leinad gave Tess intense training in the solitude of the forested hills. Their preferred training arena was at the river, where the sounds of a nearby waterfall mixed with the rhythmic clang of their swords. Tess learned quickly, and Leinad was amazed at her aptitude for the more difficult maneuvers.

It would take time, but she was the best student he'd ever had.

LEINAD AND TESS WERE FREQUENT guests at Quinn's palace. Over the following months, Quinn began courting a wealthy lady from another city. The people were pleased, and soon the invitations were sent for a wedding ball to be held in the great palace hall.

The week prior to the wedding was full of festival and celebration. Lady Moradiah brought fifty of her personal knights with her to Chessington as well as many attendants and friends.

Leinad rejoiced with his friend, but something disquieted his spirit, and he was reserved in his participation in the festivities. Though celebration was in the air, Leinad's heart became heavy.

"My dear friend, Leinad!" Quinn exclaimed as Leinad entered the great hall during the final preparations. They embraced for a moment.

"It is good to see you, Quinn," Leinad said with as much smile as he could muster.

"And you! Are you enjoying the celebrations?"

"Of course. It looks like your wedding will be the event of the decade. Quinn..." Leinad hesitated.

"I know that look, Leinad. Tell me what is on your mind."

Quinn put his arm around Leinad and pulled him into a walk down the great hall. Tomorrow was the day, and the hall was decorated with vibrantly colored banners, flowers, and greenery. Tables were being prepared with regal cloths and ornate centerpieces.

"Does Moradiah have a heart for the King?" Leinad asked.

"Of course she does," Quinn said with a broad smile. "No, no." He stopped and spoke to a servant. "The musical instruments will be over there. Move that table and prepare it." Quinn turned back to face Leinad. "I hope you will not have such a heavy heart on my wedding day, dear friend."

Leinad smiled slightly.

Moradiah entered the far end of the hall with some servants following her. She issued some orders, and they quickly became busy arranging various items in the hall.

"Moradiah, come and greet our friend, Leinad."

She approached them with all the grace of a queen. She was very beautiful. Leinad bowed and lightly kissed the hand she offered him.

"Hello, Leinad." Her voice was appealing and slightly lower in tone than most ladies. She smiled and dropped her gaze to Leinad's feet. Then she slowly brought her eyes up to meet his.

Leinad blushed slightly. "My lady," he said with a nod. She made him uncomfortable in more ways than one.

"I trust you are enjoying yourself?" she asked.

"How could one not enjoy all the celebration that surrounds us," Leinad said. "I must be on my way, however. I am due for a lesson with the knights."

"We shall see you tomorrow then," Quinn said.

On his way out of the palace, Leinad passed two of Lady Moradiah's personal knights. He nodded a greeting, but they only glared at him in return. They were fierce-looking men. Life was about to change in Chessington. Leinad could feel it.

THE POMP AND CEREMONY of the next day were beyond anything the people had ever experienced. The Knights of Chessington were dressed in their regal apparel, and the ladies wore gowns that were the envy of country wild-flowers. Even Tess wore a beautiful gown that framed her true beauty. For most, the day was a celebration of grand proportions.

The wedding was grandiose and took place in the early afternoon. Afterward, the palace, the square, and most of the city were filled with music, dancing, food, and drink. In the palace hall, the celebration continued for hours, and Leinad did his best to appear celebratory.

Toward evening, he left the hall to search for some solitude. He passed four of Lady Moradiah's knights and three giggling young ladies. The effects of strong wine enticed them to folly. Leinad found some retreat in the palace garden. His smile faded, and the heaviness he was fighting returned.

A few moments later, his thoughts were interrupted by a familiar gentle voice.

"What is bothering you, Leinad?"

Tess gracefully walked toward Leinad. He turned to greet her and suddenly became aware of how beautiful she was. It was rare to see her wearing such an elegant gown. Her long hair was loosed from the braid she usually wore, and it flowed freely around her shoulders. Though she was not primped and fitted with expensive jewelry like the rest of the ladies, she did not need it. The kindness and loyalty in her heart radiated more beauty than any exterior ornamental trappings. For a moment, Leinad felt strange inside.

"You look beautiful, Tess," he said somewhat dazed.

Tess blushed and lowered her eyes.

"I'm sorry…I didn't mean to…" he stammered.

"It's all right, Leinad. Thank you," she said and gently touched his arm. "Are you all right?"

Leinad looked away. "No, Tess. I can't shake this feeling of dread. Something is wrong. I don't trust Moradiah or her knights."

"Yes, I feel it too," Tess said. "But what can be done?"

"I don't know. I've talked to Quinn a number of times, but I'm afraid he has become blinded by his love for Moradiah."

"She makes me the most uncomfortable of all," Tess said with a slight scowl on her face.

Leinad felt reaffirmed by Tess, but he did not like to see her as troubled as he was.

"Say, I haven't had the pleasure of dancing with you yet. May I?" He held out his arm for her.

She smiled and took his arm. "I'd be delighted."

On their way back to the hall, the four knights of Moradiah accosted them.

"Hey, pretty lady, why don't you come and spend some time with us?" one asked in a repulsive manner. The others laughed.

"Watch your manners, gentlemen!" Leinad said.

"We'll do as we please with you or the lady," the knight said, emboldened by the wine in his blood and the number of his friends. They reached for their swords.

Leinad stepped between the men and Tess. "Your words dishonor the lady, the Code, and the King!"

"Your Code and your King we do not have nor do we want, but give us the lady and you may pass without feeling the steel of our swords!"

They began to draw their swords, but before the tips had cleared their scabbards, Leinad's sword was at the throat of the leader. Shock was on his face for the speed at which Leinad responded to their threat. The four of them froze with swords half-drawn.

"Return your swords and disband, or your friend will find it difficult to swallow any more wine," Leinad said.

The leader nodded slightly against the sharp edge of Leinad's blade, and the others backed away and disappeared down the hall. Leinad withdrew his sword from the throat of the man but did not sheath it. The man scowled at Leinad and retreated down the hallway.

Leinad turned and faced Tess. There was no fear in her eyes, just deep concern.

"The problem with wearing a gown is that it clashes with a sword," she said.

In THE GREAT HALL, SPEECHES and toasts were being offered. Quinn offered one to the everlasting love he had for his new bride. He encouraged her to speak a toast of her own.

"The city of Chessington is truly a great city," she said

Acclamations of "Hear, hear!" rang throughout the hall.

"And I am honored to be a part of your noble heritage. Your lord, my husband—" Moradiah reached for Quinn, and he took her hand with a smile on his lips—"is the greatest lord in the entire kingdom!"

More acclamations followed. She reveled in the praise.

"Together we will build a kingdom that will span from coast to coast. My knights will join yours, and the power of

Chessington will be unmatched by any army in history." Her voice rose in volume to bring emphasis to her words. "I will be queen, and Quinn will be king!"

All of the people in the hall rose to their feet in cheers, roused by the spirited words of Moradiah. Quinn stood with his new wife, and they raised their hands in self-glorification.

"No!" came the powerful voice of one man. "Quinn, this is blasphemous!" Leinad shouted above the rest of the noise.

The hall became hushed, and Moradiah's beautiful face turned to fierce anger at his rebuttal.

"There is only one King in Arrethtrae!" All of Leinad's restraint was broken by Moradiah's words. His zeal for the Code and for the King empowered his words and thoughts. "The knights of Moradiah do not follow the Code and do not serve the King. To join them to us is against all we believe in and work for!"

Moradiah's anger turned to rage. "My knights are mighty and strong. They do not need the Code to build an empire for us, and they can quiet your insolent tongue as well!"

Quinn tried to soothe both Leinad and Moradiah but to no avail.

"Bring your best to the square tomorrow," Leinad said. "Let the people judge whether the King's sword is able to overcome the treachery of your knights!"

"They will be there!" Moradiah exclaimed.

Leinad and Tess left the hall as Quinn tried to recapture the festive spirit of the wedding celebration. Leinad paused on the steps outside the palace and looked at its magnificent structure. Tess stopped beside him. Fury was in his eyes.

"For the love of a woman he has turned his back on the King and the Code," Leinad said. "Now he leads the people astray as well. The golden days in Chessington are over, Tess."

Darkness fell upon Chessington that night. It was a darkness that would eventually fill the lives of all.

CHAPTER SEVEN

KERGON AND THE KESSONS

 The next afternoon, Leinad rode into the square and dismounted. It was already nearly full of people. Leinad walked to the center of the square, where a young oak tree had recently been planted.

Audric and Tess were waiting, concern written on their faces. Leinad was relieved that Tess did not try to talk him out of facing Moradiah's knights. He knew she understood that it was more than a contest between men; it was a contest between principles and beliefs. Those are the battles worth fighting for since they determine the future of peoples, cities, and kingdoms.

Moradiah and her knights arrived shortly thereafter, but Quinn was absent. No matter the outcome, he would stand to lose the most, and Leinad suspected his absence signified the anguish in his heart.

As Leinad went to address Moradiah, Tess and Audric joined him with swords at their sides.

Leinad stopped. "I will not allow you to jeopardize your lives. This contest is the King's, not yours."

"You are a servant of the King, and so are we," Tess said. "Therefore, the contest is ours as well."

Leinad sighed and crossed his arms over his chest. "Please withdraw. I need to face them alone in order to stay focused. You will only hinder me." He felt bad saying these words, but he did not want them to be hurt because of his challenge.

Audric placed his hand on Leinad's shoulder. "Give the word, and we will be at your side."

Leinad was thankful for his faithful friends and wondered if they were the only ones in all of Chessington who would stand with him that day. Tess and Audric withdrew, and Leinad faced Moradiah and her fierce knights alone.

"I fight for the King and for the Code He gave us to live by. My sword is His sword. My life is His life. Without the King and without the Code, the sword will ultimately bring destruction to those who wield it. Thus the challenge is given!"

Moradiah's knights were more thugs than knights. Leinad wondered how many raids they themselves had instigated. Whether thugs or knights, they were large, muscular, and no doubt skilled with the sword.

Moradiah spoke. "Beloved people of Chessington! Leinad has robbed you of the pleasures of life for far too long. This King and the Code he speaks of are but a fairy tale meant to keep you under his control and to keep you from enjoying life without restraint. I will free you! The death of Leinad will initiate the beginning of a new age in

Chessington...an age of enticing life like you have never experienced before!"

The people seemed taken with Moradiah. Though angered, Leinad was amazed at how Moradiah's words flowed like sweet honey from the comb. He could tell that they were like delicious morsels to most of the people listening.

Leinad drew his sword, and the first knight engaged him. Leinad was too angry to play the gentleman. The knight's blows were hard but reckless. Leinad attacked with great speed and precision. Within a moment, the knight was kneeling on the ground, bleeding from his side and unable to continue. He cursed at Leinad, still unwilling to yield in his defeat.

Leinad turned to face Moradiah's next ruthless knight. She did not seem concerned and motioned for him to engage Leinad. Again Leinad quickly defeated the knight, but it was soon clear that he faced not only the skill of the knights, but also the conniving strategy of an ambitious and wicked woman. Each knight was stronger and more skilled than the previous. Moradiah was saving her best knights for last, thus allowing them to study Leinad at length while he expended the best of his energies on the weaker knights.

Although Leinad had no doubt that it was Moradiah's intent not only to defeat him but also to kill him, he did not kill his defeated foes. Those he could not disarm, he wounded enough to incapacitate them. It was not in his heart to needlessly kill, not even these scoundrels.

The fights wore on until only two of Moradiah's knights

remained. Three abandoned swords lay on the ground from the previous duels.

Moradiah was clearly becoming agitated as each of her knights was removed from the courtyard to be bandaged. She called the last two knights over and spoke a few hushed words to them.

When the first knight came to face Leinad, hatred burned in his eyes. They engaged, and their swords flew with tremendous speed and power. Leinad blocked a cut from the left with the flat of his sword and countered with a cut from the right. The knight blocked Leinad's sword and followed with a quick thrust toward Leinad's chest. Leinad parried at the last moment, but the tip of the sword cut his tunic on the left shoulder.

Leinad was tiring, and he knew that this man was fresh and fueled by the words of hatred Moradiah had spoken in his ears. Leinad refocused his thoughts and called on his final reserves of strength.

The knight could not withstand the onslaught of incredibly swift cuts and blows brought down upon him. He was in full retreat and stumbled backward to the ground just as Leinad heard a warning cry.

"Behind you, Leinad!" Tess screamed and drew her sword, but she was too far from the fight to impede the last knight, who was attacking Leinad from behind. Moradiah had signaled him to engage Leinad even though the current duel was not over. It was a treacherous attempt to win at any cost.

Leinad turned his head just in time to see a deadly cut speeding toward him from behind. In an instant, he fell to the ground and rolled on his back. The sword passed above Leinad as he rolled behind the attacking knight. Leinad maintained his momentum and pushed off the ground with his hands to catapult him into a standing position.

The knight recovered from his missed cut, turned about, and quickly brought another slice across Leinad's chest. Leinad had fully regained his feet in time to block the slice and executed a quick combination that put the knight on the defensive.

The knight that had previously stumbled to the ground regained his feet and was behind the knight that Leinad now engaged. Leinad knew he could not afford to engage both knights simultaneously, especially if they bracketed him with one on each side. At least now they were both in his direct view.

At Leinad's feet lay a sword from one of the previous duels. He deftly transferred his sword to his left hand, then placed the toe of his right foot beneath the blade of the sword on the ground and flipped it into the air. He grabbed the sword out of the air with his right hand and quickly spun full circle to his right. The sword in his right hand gained tremendous momentum through the spinning maneuver. As the tip of the sword arced around and approached the direction of the knights, he released it with deadly accuracy. It flew with the speed of an arrow released from a bow.

The closest knight just barely dodged it. The second knight, however, could not see the deadly projectile until it was too late. The sword penetrated his right shoulder to halfway up the blade. The knight dropped his sword and screamed in agony. He stumbled away from the fight and fell to the ground on one knee while clutching his wounded shoulder with his left hand.

Leinad now focused on the remaining knight. In one swift movement, he executed a powerful bind on the knight's sword, and it flew out of his hand and into the air. Leinad charged to put the man in retreat and grabbed the sword before it fell to the ground. The knight, Moradiah, and the people stood still, stunned expressions on their faces.

Leinad now held both swords as he walked toward Moradiah, who looked angry yet fearful as he approached her. Leinad stood before her, his jaw clenched and his nostrils flaring. He threw the knight's sword at her feet in contempt. She responded with a sneer, then turned in a huff and strutted back to the palace.

"Let this contest be a testimony to the truth of the Code and of the King," Leinad said to the people. "The smooth words of Moradiah are blasphemy and will bring destruction to Arrethtrae, Chessington, and your very homes if you believe them. You know what is right...you must choose!"

The people were somber. Leinad could not read them well that day. He knew that some were loyal to the King, but his heart remained heavy in spite of his victory.

Leinad, Tess, and Audric mounted their horses.

"The King reigns!" he proclaimed, and they left the square.

OVER THE NEXT YEAR, Leinad felt Moradiah's influence over the people strengthen. He was no longer a guest at the palace. At first, he fought her influence, but the people seemed bent on believing her eloquent words, and they eventually sank into a lifestyle of reckless, pleasure-filled living.

Quinn became a shell of his former self under Moradiah's overbearing, crafty, and manipulative ways.

The selfishness of the people soon began to wreak havoc on the community. The ways of the Code became archaic and foolishness to those who loved to please themselves. In their abundance and security, the people and the Knights of Chessington became lazy and apathetic. They did not realize how vulnerable they had become because of their drift from the Code and from the ways of the King.

Through it all, Tess stayed by Leinad's side, and Audric stayed true to the King and remained noble in his efforts to fulfill the Code as one of the Knights of Chessington. He was an invaluable source of inside information for Leinad.

Most of the people, however, grew to despise Leinad because he was a constant reminder of their failure to honor the King.

Although he was sorely disappointed and heavy-hearted, Leinad cared for the people because he knew that the King cared for them. Occasionally he rode into the square and spoke to as many of the people as would listen. At first they would gather to hear him, but now they gathered to chastise him.

"People of Chessington, listen to the words of the King!" he pleaded one day.

A small crowd quickly grew in size to ridicule the ranting of a man consumed with the heretical babble of the Code and the King. Tess stood off to the side.

"Destruction is at the threshold of Chessington. The King's wrath has turned His arm of protection away from you. Return to the ways of the Code!" he implored.

"Go away, Leinad. The Code and the King are a farce. We don't want any more of your talk!" the people cried.

"Have you already forgotten how the King delivered you from slavery under the hand of Fairos?" Leinad asked. "Have you forgotten how He brought you to the Chessington Valley? We prosper because of the King. We will be enslaved again because you have turned away from Him. Come back to the Code and to the ways of the King before it is too late!"

The first piece of rotten fruit flew from the crowd. Soon the jeers and the rotten food were too much. Leinad and Tess mounted their horses and left Chessington.

TESS RODE IN SILENCE BESIDE him for a long distance. She knew that the warnings to the people were over and that Leinad felt he had failed the King. What she did not know was how to encourage Leinad to care again...about anything.

Over the last year, Tess had become a master with the sword under Leinad's tutelage. It was training they both thoroughly enjoyed. It was a release from the depressing collapse of the integrity and loyalty of the people.

As dusk crept into the day, Leinad and Tess stopped. They built a fire and roasted some game, which they ate in silence.

Leinad stared into the fire.

"Why do you stay with me, Tess, when no one else will?" he finally asked.

"Because I know that what you say is true. I believe in the King as much as you do, Leinad."

Leinad looked up from the mesmerizing flames and saw the fire's reflection in her eyes. He managed a half smile.

"If only the people had just a fraction of your heart, Chessington would stand like a rock against a raging storm," he said. "But I fear their destruction is near, and I can't do a thing about it." Leinad returned his gaze to the fire. "All of them have turned away...save Audric and you."

LEINAD'S SLEEP THAT NIGHT was fitful. His final dream was of a small child playing near the edge of a cliff. The father was running to the child, but he was too far away to reach her in time. He shouted for Leinad to help the child to safety, and so Leinad ran to save her. But his legs were heavy and slow to move. The child continued to play dangerously close to the treacherous edge, unconcerned with Leinad's shouts of warning. Just as she began to slip and fall over the edge, she called out *Leinad! Leinad!*

"Leinad, wake up!" Tess whispered. She shook his shoulder. "There's a man in the trees!"

Leinad immediately rose and drew his sword. "Where?" he asked, trying to see in the early morning light.

"There!" she pointed.

A large form mounted on a horse was in the shadows of the surrounding trees. Leinad scanned the rest of the area for others but found none. He and Tess approached the form with swords ready. While still some distance away, the man spoke.

"Leinad, Chessington will soon be under attack by the powerful army of the Kessons."

"Who are you?" Leinad asked, still unable to see the man's face clearly.

"The King wants you to inform Quinn not to fight. If they fight the Kessons, many people will be killed unnecessarily. Kergon is a formidable foe, but he is merciful to those who surrender."

Leinad strained to see through the shadows. The size of the man led Leinad to believe he belonged to the King's secret force. He was a Silent Warrior.

"For seventy weeks, the King will allow the people to be taken captive because of the hardness of their hearts. Do not be discouraged. The King will be with you. One day, Gabrik will deliver a message to you from the King that will change Arrethtrae forever. You will be the messenger of hope for the people!"

The man turned his horse deeper into the trees and disappeared. Leinad did not question his identity any longer…his words were too true and too familiar to be considered a mockery.

"Let's go, Tess!" Leinad said. "Chessington needs us."

They rode their horses hard back to Chessington. The city was alive with its daily activities and business. *These people are on the precipice of disaster,* Leinad thought, *and they do not know it.*

Leinad and Tess rode straight to the palace. Though the palace guards knew that Moradiah despised Leinad, he still found favor in Quinn's eyes, and the guards granted them entrance, especially after Leinad told them his message was urgent.

Inside the palace, Leinad and Tess waited in the great hall while a servant summoned Quinn. He came quickly and greeted them with a nervous smile. The three of them had not been together for many months. Leinad thought Quinn did not look as noble as he once had. Though his apparel was regal and his actions were those of a castle lord, his eyes revealed the defeat and the submission of a knight without the spirit of the Code.

"Leinad, Tess, it is good to see you," Quinn said. They exchanged embraces.

"Quinn, I am here to warn you of impending disaster," Leinad said.

Quinn lost his smile, for he knew that Leinad was a serious man.

"As we speak, there is a great army approaching Chessington. Kergon and the Kessons intend to take the city and all its spoils."

Quinn searched Leinad's face, and then he turned away and ran his hand through his hair.

"How do you know this?" he asked, still facing away from Leinad and Tess.

"A messenger from the King."

Quinn turned back with a spark of fire in his eyes.

"Then the King sends help?" he asked hopefully.

"No, Quinn," Leinad said. "He will allow this because we have turned our backs on Him and on the Code."

Leinad felt the anger rising within him, but his compas-

sion for his friend helped diminish it. Quinn's hopeful countenance turned to consternation.

"Then we will fight them by ourselves!" he said.

"No, Quinn! The King warned that you should not fight.
You will lose, and many people will die unnecessarily."

"What?" Quinn said. "You expect me to welcome these
invaders into Chessington with open arms, to let my people
be taken as slaves, to let them ransack this beautiful city
and destroy all we have worked for?" Quinn's voice was rising in accord with his anger. "No, I will not! I am Lord
Quinn of Chessington, and I will not let Kergon or anyone
else destroy my city and enslave my people!"

Quinn turned and strode away in fury.

"Quinn!" Leinad shouted after him. Quinn stopped and
looked back at Leinad.

"This is not your city, and these are not your people."
Leinad opened his arms before him as if to encompass the
city of Chessington. "They are the King's!"

A moment of realization crossed Quinn's face, and he
softened slightly. The moment passed, however, and Quinn
turned and resumed his quickened gait.

"Guards!" he shouted.

Moradiah entered the hall and asked him what the concern was, but Quinn walked past her and exited the great
hall without speaking a word to her. She glared at Leinad
from the far end of the hall, and then exited behind Quinn.

Leinad and Tess stayed in the great hall contemplating
what to do next. A few moments later, the palace was in the
throes of feverish war preparations. Audric came into the
great hall and greeted Leinad and Tess.

"Hello, friends," he said quietly.

"Audric, you must leave Chessington," Leinad said.

Audric looked at Leinad sadly. "You know I can't, Leinad. That is not what you trained me to be."

"Then do not fight the Kessons, or you will die, my friend, and I did not train you to needlessly die."

"I took an oath that you did not, Leinad. As a Knight of Chessington, I swore to protect the city and Lord Quinn from all enemies. I do not have the luxury of annulling that oath, nor would I if it were possible. You know that my allegiance is to the King, but as long as Quinn lives, I am bound to protect him as well."

Leinad knew it was pointless to pursue the issue any further. Audric was a man of his word. It would be easier to crumble the walls of a castle single-handedly than to change his mind.

"Watch your back, Audric," Leinad said and embraced his large friend.

"You too, my friend," Audric replied. "Forgive my haste, but I must leave to prepare the Knights of Chessington for battle."

Leinad turned to Tess as Audric hurried out of the great hall. "You need to get out of the city now…and I won't take no for an answer."

Tess looked at him and slowly crossed her arms. She did not say a word, but neither did she move.

"I can't leave the people, Tess. You know that. But it is foolish for you to be taken too. You must leave!"

"I can fight better than any of the knights here. You need me," she said.

"I am not going to fight, Tess."

"Then why are you staying?"

"Because I know the King wants me with them wherever they may be…even in slavery."

Just then a company of ten knights entered the hall as if on an errand of urgency. Leinad and Tess stepped aside to let them pass, but instead the knights grabbed them and confiscated their swords.

"What's the meaning of this?" Leinad asked angrily.

"By order of Lady Moradiah, you are being held as prisoners of the palace and charged with treason against the city of Chessington." The leader of the knights stated the charge matter-of-factly. He was one of Moradiah's personal knights who had come to Chessington with her.

"This is preposterous! Take me to Quinn!"

"Silence!" the knight shouted. "Take them to the prison cells."

Leinad and Tess were taken to the lower level of the palace where the prison cells were located and thrown into one of the compartments. The heavy door was shut and locked.

"I guess neither one of us will be leaving the city," Tess said as she sat on the floor and leaned against the wall.

Leinad checked the strength of the door and then sat on the cold rock floor next to her.

"And the young child falls off the cliff," Leinad said.

"What?"

"I'm sorry, Tess. I'm sorry for the hardship of our past, and I'm sorry for the hardship of our future." Leinad leaned his head against the wall. "You deserve so much better."

Tess placed a gentle hand on his arm. "I'm not sorry, Leinad. I wouldn't change a day of my life after I met you and your father."

Leinad smiled as he remembered that day long ago when the world seemed brighter. He looked at the slender, pretty face of his companion and remembered the freckles and dirty strawberry-blond hair of her childhood. His anguish for the people of Chessington subsided for a few moments as they reminisced.

TIME PASSED SLOWLY, AND THE thick walls of the cell insulated them from the fierce battle that ensued above. Leinad and Tess mourned for the people and for the city. Many hours later, a servant boy came running down the stairs with keys jingling in his hands. Soon the door of their cell was opened, and Leinad and Tess exited quickly.

"I know you are good people, and I have seen the wickedness of Moradiah firsthand," the boy said.

"Thank you, son," Leinad said. "You have done well. How goes the battle?"

"The city is nearly overrun. Most of the knights are dead, and the Kessons are approaching the palace as we speak." The boy looked down. "It is awful, Sir Leinad."

Leinad put his hand on the boy's shoulder. "What of Lord Quinn and Lady Moradiah?"

"Lord Quinn leads the battle on the steps of the palace. Lady Moradiah tried to flee, but the Kessons pursued. She is dead, sir."

"Where did they put our swords, son?"

"I don't know, sir. I think they were taken to the armory."

"Do you know what my sword looks like?"

The boy smiled. "Yours is the grandest of them all, Sir Leinad."

Leinad knelt down to face the boy eye-to-eye. "Do me a favor, lad. Find my sword and stow it in a safe place. Do you know of a safe place?"

The boy ran into the cell that Leinad and Tess had been in and slid a brick loose from one of the corners. A dirt alcove that was deep enough for a sword lay behind the brick.

"For a young boy, you sure seem to know a lot about this palace," Leinad said with a slight smile.

"Nobody pays much attention to a servant boy, so I know a lot more than most folk realize."

Leinad put his hand on the boy's shoulder. "If you can't find my sword quickly, find someplace out of the way and stay put until the fighting is over, all right?"

"Yes, sir."

Leinad and Tess hurried up the prison stairs, and the sounds of deadly fighting filled the air.

The Kessons were at the palace gates and were overrunning the few remaining knights. Quinn and twenty or so knights were heavily engaged in a last stand on the palace steps. Leinad spotted Audric at the front of the line beside Quinn. It was a desperate battle.

Leinad looked for a sword so he could join the fray, but there was none.

Quinn fought with more courage and valor than Leinad

had ever seen in him. It was as though he fought to cover the mistakes he'd made…against the people and against the King.

Two Kessons engaged him at the same time, and it was too much. Audric tried to cover Quinn's side, but a sword was thrust into his abdomen, and Quinn fell backward onto the granite steps.

"No!" Leinad shouted as he ran down the palace steps to his fallen comrade.

A man on horseback rode up in full battle attire. The air of command was in him. "Do you yield?" he shouted.

The Knights of Chessington fell back, and the fighting paused in response to Kergon's question.

Leinad knelt beside Quinn and lifted his head slightly. Leinad held his hand over the wound.

Quinn coughed and winced at the pain. He grabbed Leinad's tunic. "Leinad," he gasped, "tell the King I am sorry. Tell Him I was wrong. I wanted to be a good leader for the people."

"You were a good leader, Quinn," Leinad said as tears welled up in his eyes.

The agony on Quinn's face eased slightly, and then he fell limp in Leinad's arms.

The silent moment of mourning that followed was interrupted by Kergon's strong voice once again.

"Do you yield?"

Leinad let Quinn's head come to rest on the steps and then stood to face Kergon.

"We yield."

Leinad looked out across Chessington. The once beautiful city was now a battle scene engulfed in flames. Cries and screams reached Leinad's ears, and the tears in his eyes were not just for Quinn now.

"Please have mercy on the people, Lord Kergon. There has been enough death for today," Leinad said.

Kergon nodded, and the killing ceased.

BY DAY'S END, CHESSINGTON lay in ruins, and most of the people were gathered into a slave march to the land of the Kessons—to the city of Daydelon. The chains of bondage were latched once more onto the limbs of the people. It was the beginning of another dark chapter in the lives of the King's people.

CHAPTER EIGHT

KERGON'S CAPTIVES

Kergon left one of his top men in Chessington to rule the city and surrounding areas for him. Although nearly all of the inhabitants of Chessington were sent on the march to Daydelon, Kergon allowed a handful to remain in the city as subjects of his newly established lord. Most of these were the older people that Kergon did not think would survive the journey. Anyone with any influence or authority was taken, and thus Leinad, Tess, and Audric found themselves on a trek into bondage once again.

The march to Daydelon was arduous. Although the terrain itself was not difficult, harsh weather during the three-week journey took a tremendous toll on the unsheltered people. Hard rains and cold nights resulted in many illnesses and even some deaths. Even though enslavement lay within the walls of Daydelon, the people were relieved to finally arrive at the end of their tortuous voyage.

The city of Daydelon was an incredible sight to behold. In all of his days, Leinad had never seen such a magnificent feat of design and construction. A formidable wall encompassed the entire city, which straddled the river that supplied fresh water to the inhabitants. Both inside and outside the wall, lush vegetation embraced the monolithic stone structure. Vibrant gardens adorned the city streets, squares, and palace. Were it not for the rule of Kergon and the plight of the slaves, Daydelon would have appeared to be a paradise.

Once within the walls, the people were taken to a servant preparation area. The men were divided from the women and children, and Leinad was troubled at the thought of not being able to protect Tess. He reminded himself that she was as tough as any knight he'd known. He would have to protect her through the training he had given her. These thoughts helped—a little.

Over the next week, slave auctions were held to sell the people off to the highest bidders. Kergon profited greatly from the slave market. It was as beneficial as the taxes he collected, and his wealthy citizens loved to participate. Slaves were an integral part of the Kessons' economic, social, and labor structure. Of course Kergon reserved first choice for himself, and he chose Leinad, among others, to serve in the palace.

Leinad wondered if he would ever see Tess or Audric again.

THE DAYS BECAME WEEKS, the weeks became months, and the months became a year. Though the bondage for the

King's people was much more bearable than what they had experienced under Fairos in Nyland, they longed to be free and return to Chessington. Leinad knew that the King was aware of their predicament, and so he encouraged the people whenever he could.

Leinad's service to Kergon changed over the months. At first he was kept under close supervision and performed hard manual labor. But as he proved himself trustworthy, Kergon's captain gave him more and more responsibility and freedom. One of his duties included organizing the purchases required to maintain palace operations. Through these contacts, Leinad learned that Tess had been sold to a wealthy widow who was sympathetic to young ladies up for sale in a city that was less than scrupulous in its treatment of slaves. Though he hadn't seen Tess since their arrival in the city, he was relieved that she was in a moderately safe environment.

One day, Leinad was inspecting a number of carts loaded with produce that was to be delivered to the palace. Two other palace servants accompanied him. The shop owner bragged incessantly about the quality of his produce, and Leinad was becoming annoyed with the man.

"You will not find produce as fine as this in all of Daydelon," the shop owner said with a smile as he followed Leinad through the inspection. A contract to sell goods to the palace was envied by most merchants.

"I'm sure your goods are top quality," Leinad said. "But I must inspect them thoroughly anyway."

The shop was in the central part of Daydelon called the Market, where the gentle sound of the river mixed with the daily routine of market activity. By night, the river's flow was a gentle, soothing lullaby to those near enough to hear it. Large trees and shrubs lined the streets and walkways. The Market was clean and neat and a delightful place to conduct business. On a day like today, with the sun shining bright in the blue sky, the streets were teeming with activity.

Leinad stepped around the shop owner to advance to the next cart and bumped into a finely dressed woman inspecting an intricate dining plate. The plate fell to the ground and shattered into a hundred pieces.

"Oh, I am so sorry, my lady," Leinad said as he knelt down to gather the broken pieces. He hoped that she was not a lady of importance in the city, for such an incident with a slave could be disastrous.

"You're going to pay for that!" the shop owner screamed as he exited the shop.

Leinad continued to work at gathering the pieces. "The expense is mine," he said. The shop owner arrived at the scene red-faced and angry.

"How much was the dish?" Leinad asked.

The shop owner stated a price that Leinad knew was probably twice its value, but he reached for the palace money bag and hoped he could explain himself to Kergon's treasury officer.

"Thank you, Lady Weldon," Leinad heard the shop owner say politely as he fumbled to open the bag.

The woman paid the shop owner, and he disappeared back into his shop.

Hardly daring to look the woman in the eye, Leinad thanked her. He knew she must be a prominent woman by the shop owner's response.

"Please forgive me, my lady," Leinad said and bowed.

"It's quite all right, young man," she said. "Just be a little more careful when you're about your business." Her speech was refined and dignified. "Tess, come along," she called into the shop.

Leinad nearly fell over at the mention of Tess's name. He raised himself up and turned to see Tess exiting the same shop. His heart leapt within his chest at seeing her, for it had been over a year since they were last together.

She was dressed in fine clothing and looked like a lady of stature herself. She stopped midstride and astonishment overcame her. Her eyes widened and her mouth parted slightly, but quickly transformed into a jubilant smile.

"Leinad!" she exclaimed and ran to him.

They embraced, and Leinad felt true joy in his heart for the first time since their enslavement. Somehow he knew it was true for Tess as well. They stepped back from one another as if to convince themselves that they were truly together again, even if it was for just a moment.

"Tess, is it really you?" Leinad said with wonder. He never would have believed that the freckle-faced little girl of Mankin would grow up to be the lovely, refined woman that stood before him.

"So this is the young man you spoke of so glowingly," Lady Weldon said.

"Lady Weldon, please meet Sir Leinad of Chessington," Tess said with pride and dignity in her voice.

Leinad bowed a second time to Lady Weldon and was amazed at how polished Tess's speech had become.

"I am pleased to meet you, Sir Leinad," Lady Weldon said.

"The pleasure is mine, my lady," Leinad said as he finished bowing.

"I have some unfinished business in the shop across the street. Tess, join me after a bit."

"Yes, my lady," she said with a smile that radiated delight and appreciation.

Leinad turned to one of the other servants and asked him to finish the inspection for him.

Tess put her arm through Leinad's. "Shall we take a walk, sir?" she asked sweetly.

Leinad smiled and led them toward a walkway that skirted the river. It was odd for him to see his sword-fighting companion as a poised and dignified young lady. It was apparent that Lady Weldon had given Tess what Leinad and his father never could. His feelings and his words felt awkward to him at first. It was like getting to know her for the first time.

"Enslavement has suited you well, Sunshine," he said.

She dropped her smile. "Too well, Leinad. Look at me. Although I am a servant at her estate, Lady Weldon treats us more like daughters than slaves. I am spoiled and feel guilty when I see the plight of our people. It is difficult for me to come to the Market like this, but Lady Weldon occasionally insists. It has been months since my last visit."

Leinad placed his hand on Tess's hand that held his arm. "Of all people, Tess, you should not feel guilty about being treated well, and I am glad you came to the Market today."

She smiled, but Leinad knew that the words would not change her feelings. "Have you heard anything of Audric?" he asked.

"No, I have not. I hope he is well. Some of the people are serving under difficult masters."

"Yes, I know. With my new responsibilities at the palace, I have been able to contact many more of the people. For most, the bondage weighs heavily on them."

Tess looked down and away.

"I'm sorry, Tess. I didn't mean to—"

"It's all right. I know what's happening here. I would leave in an instant if given the chance," she said defiantly. "How long will the King leave us here, Leinad?"

"The time is not far off, Tess."

They walked and soaked up every moment they had together, for their next visit might be months away, if ever.

On their return, Leinad thanked Lady Weldon for allowing them time together and for affording Tess a safe haven in the midst of captivity. It was a day that both Leinad and Tess cherished for weeks to come. ❖

CHAPTER NINE

INTO THE JAWS OF DRAGAMOTH

Kergon continued to prosper and conquer. He became powerful in the region and in all of Arrethtrae. As Kergon's fame and influence grew, Leinad observed, so did his pride. With no force strong enough to penetrate the great city, Kergon believed the title of *King* was his to take. The lesser lords could not dispute him. They either vowed their allegiance or were overthrown.

Kergon ordained one day to confirm his crown. The palace grounds were prepared, and the boulevards were lined with all the inhabitants of the city. When the palace trumpets sounded, every man, woman, and child was to bow to demonstrate allegiance to Kergon as King of Arrethtrae.

It was a day of pomp and ceremony in the palace, but for one man, it was a day of intense sorrow. Leinad knew he could not kneel, and he was willing to accept whatever consequences fell upon him. What saddened his heart was that others would be forced to accept the same fate or

93

compromise their convictions because of the fear that surely gripped them.

Who will be strong and die…who will be weak and live? he wondered. *Oh Tess, that I could spare you this day.*

Kergon's guards were placed throughout the mass of people to maintain order and to ensure submission.

Kergon stepped onto the high balcony of his palace, which overlooked his great city, and the trumpets blew. The mass of people knelt in unison before the self-proclaimed king. All the people…except three.

"Kneel down, Tess!" Lady Weldon exclaimed.

"I am sorry, my lady. I cannot. There is only one King of Arrethtrae, and I have already sworn my allegiance to Him."

"This is something I cannot protect you from, Tess. Please kneel," Lady Weldon said softly.

Tess looked kindly on Lady Weldon. "Thank you for all you have done for me, my lady."

"Kneel or you will die!" an approaching guard shouted.

WITHIN A SHORT TIME, LEINAD, Tess, and Audric were brought before Kergon.

"It is good to see you, old friend," Leinad said quietly to Audric as they waited for Kergon to approach them. Leinad could tell by Audric's tattered clothing that his captivity had been difficult.

Audric grinned lightheartedly. "And you, my friends," he nodded.

Leinad's respect for Audric had grown tremendously over the years. He was a man of intense loyalty and convictions—two qualities Leinad found lacking in most men. The forthcoming adversity seemed easier to bear knowing that Audric and Tess were by his side. From the days of Fairos until now, they had been Leinad's faithful companions and supporters. Their devotion to the King had been steady and sure through the years. They were true Knights of the King as well. Standing tall, the three of them now faced certain death for defying Kergon's claim to be king of Arrethtrae.

Kergon left his balcony and approached them, anger burning in his eyes. He was a distinguished-looking man with a beard that held streaks of gray. He carried himself with an authority that demanded submission from all of his subjects—almost all.

At his approach, the four guards surrounding Leinad, Tess, and Audric saluted. Kergon stopped before them with his chin raised slightly.

"I am told that the three of you have refused to kneel and swear your allegiance to me as king," Kergon said with restrained anger in his voice. He stepped closer to Leinad. "You have been a faithful servant for some time now. You have earned my trust. To show you that I am a merciful king, I will allow you and these other two to kneel now so that you may live."

"Lord Kergon," Leinad said boldly, "though you give us a hundred chances, we will not kneel before you to swear our allegiance to you as king."

Kergon's face turned red. Such defiance was not thought possible in his city.

"We have sworn our allegiance to the one true King of Arrethtrae," Leinad continued. "There is not nor ever will be another."

"Then you will die, and your King can do nothing to save you!"

"You are mistaken, Lord Kergon. Our King is more than able to save us," Leinad said. "Though should He choose not to, we are prepared to die as Knights of the true King of Arrethtrae."

"Guards! Take them to the Vale of the Dragons!" Kergon commanded. "And spread fresh meat up to the tree line to entice the dragamoths!"

The guards brutishly escorted the three of them out of the presence of Kergon.

Though they had not seen the Vale of the Dragons, they knew what cruel death lay before them. The northern wall of Daydelon was higher than the other walls and bordered a large, densely forested valley. No man had ever traveled the valley, for it was inhabited by the ferocious dragamoths. Kergon utilized these beasts to his benefit. A small clearing in the valley vegetation near the wall provided a natural arena for him to feed his enemies to the dragamoths. Two extension walls were built that joined the main city wall to eliminate the possibility of escape. There was no need to bind the victims. Their only choice was to await their fate in the clearing or venture past the valley tree line into the habitat of the dragamoth—an unthinkable prospect.

Leinad, Tess, and Audric were forced to don clothing that was splattered with the blood of goats. Six guards then led them to the base of the north wall, where a large iron door was the only barrier between them and the jaws of the dragamoths.

"You have seen these dragamoths?" Leinad asked Audric.

"No, I have only been told of them."

"Tell us," Leinad said.

Audric looked sympathetically at Tess.

"I am afraid, Audric, but I am not a coward," she said. "We need to know what we will be facing."

He nodded. "It is said that the dragamoth can smell as well as a dog...thus our clothing. Most of them are half again as tall as a man, but some are said to be twice that size. They run faster than a man but slower than a horse. Their claws are long and their teeth are sharp. And..."

"Yes?" Leinad said.

"And it is said that they breathe fire."

"Fire?" Leinad asked.

Audric raised an eyebrow and tilted his head slightly to affirm his own doubt. Tess's eyes widened, and they all fell silent.

"Well, I can see why the antelope were leaping to their deaths back in the Red Canyon." Tess said. "Do you know of any weakness we can exploit?"

Audric crossed his muscular arms and took a deep breath. "It is said that they can only see movement, but without weapons and with our clothes splattered in blood, I don't see how that is going to help us much."

"Maybe not, but it's something," Tess said.

Just then a guard on horseback arrived at the gate with two slabs of fresh meat dangling from each side of his saddle. His face was white with fear.

One of the guards looked through a small hole into the clearing. "All clear!" he shouted.

Two other guards removed the iron lock and opened the doors just far enough for the guard on horseback to exit.

"Ride fast, Garth, and you'll make it," said one of the guards as he slapped the horse's back end.

The rider was gone in a bolt, and the doors were closed and locked behind him. He was back at the door a moment later. The guards opened the door and let their terrified comrade and his horse, minus the slabs of meat, back into the city.

The gate guard signaled for the other guards to bring the prisoners to the gate. As they passed, the gate guard leaned close to Leinad's ear and spoke softly. "Some of the riders did not make it back from their meat drops. You may find a sword or two near the tree line if you dare to venture that close to the abode of the dragamoths."

Leinad nodded his thanks, and the guards pushed them into the Vale of the Dragons.

Clean white bones were scattered throughout the clearing, which was quite wide. Two walls extended from the city wall well into the dense vegetation of the valley. Leinad looked up the enormous city wall and saw the tiny figure of Kergon amidst a throng of onlookers.

Leinad noticed that one slab of meat had been dropped near the tree line, which was a fair distance from the city wall. The only protection was an occasional outcropping of rocks; the second slab of meat lay near the largest outcropping.

They moved quickly but cautiously toward the rock

formation. Once there, Leinad turned and held out his hand to Audric and Tess. "It is an honor to face death in the company of two gallant knights such as you."

Audric and Tess took his handshake and nodded.

"The King reigns," Leinad said.

"The King reigns," they replied.

A hideous screech filled the air. Leinad had heard that sound only once before—in the Red Canyon. Chills flowed up his spine.

"I want you to wait here," he said.

"What are you doing?" Tess asked with a look of concern on her face.

"Wait here. I'll be back."

Leinad grabbed the fresh meat and ran toward the tree line. Another screech, much closer than the first, filled the air. Leinad scanned the ground as he ran and kept a watchful eye on the distant trees ahead.

Finally, he reached the other slab of meat near the tree line. He dropped his cargo and fervently searched the ground. He found a number of horses' bones mixed with those of men. Another terrifying screech blasted from the trees, and Leinad knew that a dragamoth was approaching fast.

He moved a pile of bones—success! A rusted sword lay beneath.

Leinad grabbed the sword and started his run back to the boulders. Off to his right he spotted the hilt of a second sword almost covered in dirt. He chanced a detour to retrieve the second sword, though he knew the extra time might cost him.

© Marcella Johnson

The thick vegetation of the tree line moved and parted. A dragamoth leapt through the opening and screeched the cry of a merciless predator.

Leinad froze with his hand on the hilt of the buried sword and his eye on the terrifying dragamoth.

The dragamoth was slender and looked built for speed. The upper and lower jaws were long and lined with razor-sharp teeth. Yellow catlike eyes gave the creature its limited sight. The base of the head terminated smoothly into a long neck that seemed to have an extra degree of motion at a joint one-third of the way toward the body. Short, powerful arms with long, ripping claws gave the dragamoth added weaponry to use against its prey. Longer muscular hind legs supported the body and gave it incredible speed for a creature of this size. Its final weapon was a long, powerful, and flexible tail. From head to tail, the dragamoth's skin was lizardlike and colored in streaks of yellow and dark brown.

The dragamoth paused and licked the air with its forked tongue, smelling the fresh meat. It moved toward the meat and swallowed one slab whole. While it was occupied with its meal, Leinad resumed his sprint back to his companions at the boulders.

The dragamoth finished the second slab of meat and resumed its hunt for more. Its eyes caught Leinad's movement, and it screeched before pursuing its next prey. Other dragamoths screeched from the valley trees, drawn by the hunt of the first.

The distance to the rock formation was too far, and Leinad knew he wouldn't make it in time. He threw one of the swords as far toward his companions as possible and turned to face the beast. It was a terrifying sight to see such a voracious beast charging at him.

Audric ran to gather the other sword, but he could not reach Leinad in time. It was a hopeless moment…or so it seemed.

The tree line moved again, but this time no dragamoth emerged. Instead, a man on a white horse charged into the clearing and raced toward the attacking dragamoth.

Stunned, Leinad simply readied his sword.

The man covered the distance to the dragamoth quickly—gleaming sword in hand. The dragamoth, intent only on Leinad, leapt into the air to pounce.

The gallant man on horseback reached him before he landed. Leinad dove to the side as the rider made one quick power cut across the neck of the dragamoth and severed its head. Its body landed with an empty thud in a limp pile where Leinad once stood.

Sounds of exclamation filtered down from the people watching on the city wall.

The man turned his horse and faced Leinad. There was something familiar about him. Leinad felt he was in the presence of the King again…but he was not the King. The man was young and possessed the perfect form of a knight's knight. His brow was noble, and his eyes burned like fire. His sword was truly magnificent, nearly identical to another that Leinad had once seen.

Who could this be? Then Leinad remembered the traveler who had helped him and Tess many years ago in the Tara Hills Mountain Range when they were starving. Was this the same man?

The man reached out his arm. Leinad recovered himself and grabbed hold as the man lifted him to the back of his horse. A moment later they were back at the rocky outcropping with Audric and Tess. They dismounted, and the man drew another sword to hand to Tess. Now all were armed.

The horse galloped to the city wall and trotted back and forth along its length, waiting for the call of his master.

Two dragamoths emerged from the tree line and descended on the fallen creature's headless body.

The gallant man turned to face Leinad, Tess, and Audric. His countenance was determined, but he evoked a strange peace that passed on to Leinad and, he was sure, to Tess and Audric as well. Somehow, Leinad knew they would make it through. There was no time to discover who the man was—they just knew that he had the skill, the wisdom, and the power to defeat these vicious creatures.

"Attack the dragamoths in teams of two," the man commanded. "One distracts while the other strikes. Aim just below the jointed neck. If that is not possible, its heart is just behind the forelegs."

Another dragamoth parted the tree line and made straight for the boulders.

"Is there fire?" Leinad asked.

"There is no fire, but it will spit a deadly acidlike poison once it realizes you are attacking it. Stay clear of the direction of the mouth."

The approaching dragamoth was larger than the other three. Its screech was lower and even more threatening than the others. It reached the rock formation and paused, perhaps deciding which prey to devour first.

The stranger positioned himself directly in front of the dragamoth, fearless and confident. His stature emanated power.

The creature snapped and swiped at the stranger with one of its claws. The stranger's sword flew with blinding speed and severed the forearm of the creature. It screeched an ear-piercing cry, and a stream of yellow fluid burst from its mouth. Its aim was poor, and the fluid splattered on the boulders behind them. Smoke rose from the boulders where the fluid landed.

Leinad ran to the creature's side and plunged his sword deep into the body just aft of the forearms. The dragamoth convulsed, and its tail whipped and struck Leinad across his side. Leinad slammed into a rock and struggled to regain his breath.

The creature fell to the ground, writhing momentarily before becoming still in death.

The cries of the dying dragamoth drew the attention of the other two beasts, who quickly advanced on the four brave warriors. Audric took up a position to fight the first one, and the stranger joined him while Tess positioned herself to face the next creature. Leinad stood to help Tess and felt an intense burning inside his chest. The pain was excruciating.

Once again, sounds of astonishment were heard from the crowd on the wall above, for no man or team of men had ever faced a dragamoth and lived, not even with weapons.

Leinad drew the dragamoth's attention away from Tess, for he knew that the strike of his sword was now weak. The dragamoth screeched and poised itself to pounce. Tess moved in quickly from the left and struck the creature with the deadly edge of her sword, but it moved at the last instant, and her blade struck the bony joint of the neck. Tess fell below the creature as it recoiled and screeched in anger. A stream of yellowish poison flew straight at Leinad. He fell to the ground and rolled, barely escaping the deadly fluid. Tess rolled to avoid the sharp claws of the powerful hind legs.

The creature lowered its head to capture Tess in its jaws. She rolled to her knees and thrust her sword past the deadly jaws and deep into its throat. The dragamoth clamped down on the sword, nearly taking Tess's arm with it. The blade penetrated clear through the neck. The dragamoth could not screech or spit as it clawed at the weapon with its front claws.

Leinad tried to stand, but the broken ribs in his chest made it impossible. "Tess! Here!" he called and threw his sword toward her.

She grabbed the sword and plunged it deep into the heart of the flailing dragamoth. The creature collapsed to the ground dead.

A moment later, Audric and the stranger killed the remaining creature. Four dragamoths lay dead in the clearing, and four warriors stood, ready for more.

"Leinad!" Kergon shouted down from the lofty heights of the wall. "Surely your King has delivered you. Return to the gate, for no man, common or noble, can do what I have seen here today."

The four quickly made their way to the gate, and the stranger mounted his horse.

"Who are you, sir?" Leinad asked.

The man looked at Leinad warmly. "I am a man from a distant land."

The stranger's horse reared, and then he bolted straight for the trees. There was no fear, no hesitation, as he rode into the Vale of the Dragons. He was like no other man the kingdom had ever seen.

THE REGATHERING

Tess and Audric were given positions in Kergon's palace with Leinad and were treated quite well. Their stewardship of Kergon's resources quickly won them additional responsibilities, authority, and some freedom. Leinad was pleased to be reunited with his companions, but his heart was still heavy with sadness for the bondage of the King's people.

Kergon's pride continued to swell along with his accumulated wealth. The city of Daydelon was the envy of the kingdom, as well as a treasured prize for the many enemies Kergon had made over the years.

Leinad often escaped for a short time to enjoy a walk along the river. On a few occasions, Tess was able to join him.

Today, Leinad had finished his duties and returned to the river that beckoned him to freedom. He stopped beside a tree that stretched its branches across the gently flowing water. He knelt beside the river's green bank. In the serenity of his surroundings, he could not help thinking about the golden days in Chessington.

His life had been a strange compilation of adventures. From the sweet days of his youth to enslavement, wandering, and finally settling in the Chessington Valley, Leinad still wondered at times what his end purpose for the King would be. Every time he helped the people forward, calamity and disaster tore at them like a hungry lion. Was this his purpose? It seemed futile, and yet he knew that the King was so much bigger than the circumstances they faced. Surely the vision Leinad's father once spoke of would be revealed, and he would discover his final purpose in the King.

As the memories of the past months flowed through his mind, he remembered the warning of the Silent Warrior in the forest outside Chessington. That had been the beginning of their captivity. But he also remembered the Silent Warrior's words about the duration of their captivity—seventy weeks. Leinad's soberness turned to anticipation when he realized that their time of captivity was nearly fulfilled.

Leinad became aware of a presence behind him. He turned to see a large man kneeling beside him.

"Leinad," the man said in a hushed tone while staring into the water, "tonight Daydelon will be overtaken. You must get word to the people to stay within their homes. Tell them not to fight, for Kergon's enemies have no quarrel with the King's people. They do not want slaves; they want the wealth of the city and to kill Kergon. Tomorrow you will all be free."

The man promptly stood and left without giving Leinad

any opportunity for questions. It seemed to be the style of the King's messengers.

That night, a large and silent force gathered outside the grand gates of Daydelon. A smaller force of men entered the river that flowed under the city wall and swam beneath the surface to gain access to the city. Once inside, they quietly overpowered the gate guards and opened the doors for the waiting army.

Kergon's slumbering army and citizens were taken, and before the break of dawn of the next day, Kergon lay dead. The mighty reign of the Kessons was over. Daydelon's precious treasures were looted, and those residents who resisted were killed.

Leinad petitioned Drasius, the commander of the conquering army, to allow his people to leave. Drasius was more than willing, for slaves were only a burden to an army looking for gold and silver.

WITHIN A FEW DAYS, MOST OF the people of Chessington were en route back to their beloved valley. Some chose to stay in Daydelon, for they had grown accustomed to the city and to the lifestyle of the Kessons.

For those who rejoiced at their freedom and longed to return home, their joy was turned to sorrow many days later when they entered the Chessington Valley and beheld their city. Chessington lay in ruins, and nothing of value remained, save the noble few who had endured the constant raids that a city without defenses invited.

Leinad felt the heaviness of his own heart and tried to overcome it with words of encouragement and promise to the people.

"People of Chessington, do not despair," he urged. "The King is with us…we are His people. One day He will bring peace to Arrethtrae. There will be no more slavery, no more fighting, no more thirsting, and no more hunger. The King did not leave us; we left the King. Let us resolve in our hearts never to leave the King again. Let us resolve to follow the Code forevermore. Let this day be known in all of Arrethtrae as the day that the people of Chessington did not falter—the day we rose above the ashes of a destroyed city and stood firm.

"Let us raise up an army of noble warriors to defend our city. Warriors who swear to follow and uphold the Code. These warriors will be called the Noble Knights and will be your protection and your guide. We will build our city again. We will stand tall in the valley once again!"

The people were moved by Leinad's passionate words and rallied on the crest of the hill that looked down into the valley. Though their road ahead would be difficult, it was theirs alone to journey.

They were a hearty people who had endured much. Their tenacity to survive against all odds had established their hearts in the King's land. Their folly had been in believing the deception of those who hated the King.

But all along, they had known the right path, and this time they believed they could follow it. 🔳

CHAPTER ELEVEN

THE PROMISE

 Once back in the city, Leinad went to the palace and descended the steps into the prison cell where he and Tess had spent most of the battle with the Kessons over a year earlier. He pulled the loose brick from the corner and hoped he would discover his treasure. There lay the beautiful sword Gabrik had given him many years before. He pulled his sword from the dirt alcove and felt whole once again.

The months passed, and Leinad was true to his word. He trained an army of noble men who were true in deed and in heart to the King and the Code. Under his masterful swordsmanship training, the Noble Knights became feared among all bandits and thieves that attempted to raid Chessington. All of these gallant men swore their allegiance to the King and to Him only. Leinad was careful to instill the principles of loyalty, honesty, integrity, courage, and humility into his training of the Noble Knights. These were the principles of the Code. These were the principles the Noble Knights lived and died by.

Chessington was now protected and was in the process of being rebuilt. It would take years to attain the glory of the golden years they had once enjoyed under Quinn's rule. However, the people persevered. It was a time to rediscover their identity with the King.

Tess and Audric were instrumental in helping Leinad restore the order of the Code and in training the Noble Knights. Tess's skill with the sword quickly won the respect of the knights. Any who might ridicule her were immediately silenced once they felt the sting of defeat beneath her swift blade. She also proved herself in battle many times against the various bands of thieves that tried to loot the city.

Leinad chose Audric to lead the Noble Knights, for his experience was the greatest among the men, and Leinad knew that his heart belonged completely to the King.

"Leinad," Audric protested when he learned of Leinad's decision, "you are the one to lead the Noble Knights, not I."

Leinad, Tess, and Audric stood in the middle of the square after a training session with the Noble Knights. The coolness of the late afternoon air marked the change of seasons in the land.

"No, Audric," Leinad said. "I will never accept the leadership of the people. It is not my mission. I will guide, admonish, and encourage them, but I will never be their ruler."

Audric crossed his arms, and his gentle eyes were partially obscured by his furrowed eyebrows. He looked as though he was seriously considering opposing a decision of Leinad's for the first time ever.

Leinad read the concern of his large friend and knew that his quiet demeanor was a deterrent to his accepting the leadership of the Noble Knights.

"Audric, you are the most experienced, the most skilled, and the most worthy of all the Noble Knights." Leinad said. "I understand your hesitation, but that is why you are perfect for the position. You are not a glory seeker. What you do will be tempered by humility, wisdom, and experience. Tess is more than capable to help train, and Kendrid can be your second, for he has won the respect of the other men as well."

"You sound as if you are going away," Tess said to Leinad with one eyebrow raised. "Is there something you're not telling us?"

Leinad paused, unsure how to respond to her keen insight. "All of this is part of the King's plan for the future of Arrethtrae." Leinad swept his hand, as if across the city of Chessington and the valley beyond. "But something is missing, and I know that somehow I must find out what it is. We have arrived at the door to a grand kingdom, but the key is missing. This key is the vision in my life that I've been searching for, Tess. Over the past months, I have realized that my mission is the quest for this key. It is what my father spoke of. He knew—and now I know—that I must find it. I feel the call of the King, but I do not know where to go." Leinad turned to Audric. "That is why you must take leadership of the Noble Knights."

Audric's attempt at a rebuttal was interrupted by the hasty approach of a mysterious rider. He rode off the main street and directly onto the square. He was dressed in full battle attire, and his size, especially atop his large powerful steed, was intimidating.

"Sir Leinad of Chessington?" he asked in a deep voice.

Leinad stepped forward. "I am Leinad."

The warrior glared at him as if to adjust his preconceived perceptions. "Sir Gabrik is in battle with the Dark Knight and his Shadow Warriors. The situation is grave, and he has dispatched me to bid you to come to him."

"Let me gather the Noble Knights, and we will come to his aid," Leinad said.

"No. The distance is too far, and Chessington will be vulnerable," the warrior said emphatically. "This is not a fight for them yet. They are not ready to fight the Dark Knight or his Shadow Warriors."

"Then how can I be of service?"

"Mount up and ride with me back to the battle."

Tess stepped forward. "I will come with you."

"This is for Leinad alone," the rider said.

Tess turned toward Leinad while not turning her back completely to the mysterious rider. "How do we know that he is not an enemy of the King and is luring you into a trap?" she asked with concern in her eyes.

"Sir Gabrik has what you search for, Sir Leinad," the rider said impatiently. "It is why he sends for you, but we have no time to spare. If Lucius overtakes our force, Chessington will not survive, and the future of Arrethtrae will be lost forever."

Leinad put his hand on Tess's shoulder and looked into her deep blue eyes. Tess was an interesting balance of beauty and warrior. She was too tough for the ladies of

Chessington but every bit as refined thanks to Lady Weldon of Daydelon. She was too lovely to be treated as one of the men of Chessington but every bit as skilled with the sword thanks to Leinad. Her allegiance was to the King, and her heart belonged secretly to another. Leinad sensed more than concern in her gaze, but the concern was what he addressed.

"I must go, Tess. It is why I am here!"

Tess stared unapologetically into his eyes and then looked at the mysterious rider. She leaned forward to speak quietly into Leinad's ear. "Watch your back, mister...and promise you'll come back to me."

Leinad struggled with the passion in her quiet voice. Their dangerous adventures of the past had stirred concern in Tess before, but somehow this was different, and Leinad felt it.

"I promise, Sunshine," he said quietly and close to her ear. "I promise." He reached down and squeezed her hand.

"I think it wise to ready the men," Audric said with a voice of command. "There is a darkness that hangs in the air."

Leinad turned to Audric and nodded to affirm the transfer of leadership. He then hurried to his horse, mounted, and followed the mysterious rider north out of Chessington in a full gallop.

THERE WAS NO TIME FOR talk on the journey. Leinad and the mysterious rider drove their horses hard, for the urgency of the battle seemed to rise as distance passed.

They continued north past Chandril. At nightfall they

stopped at a river to drink and let their mounts recover some lest they collapse from the strain of the ride. Leinad discovered there that the name of his escort was Greshane.

After a few short hours of rest, they crossed the river and pressed on toward the Northern Mountains, where few men journeyed and fewer lived. At the foothills of the mountain range, Greshane slowed their pace to a quiet trot and finally to a walk. At one point, in a heavily forested area, he stopped their advance completely and held his hand up for silence. Leinad listened and watched, but there was nothing out of the ordinary that his experienced senses could detect. Greshane was finally satisfied as well but still spoke softly.

"Dismount. We can travel more easily through the dense trees on foot. We are close to our encampment, but the Shadow Warriors are close as well. I am not sure what has transpired in my absence. I hope we are not too late."

"Why is there fighting now?" asked Leinad after dismounting.

"There is always fighting, but the foretelling must be given. The Dark Knight and his warriors know that something significant in the King's plan is about to happen, but they do not know what. Thus they—"

The forest seemed to collapse upon them in a blaze of flashing swords and a spine-chilling battle cry from the throats of a six massive warriors...Shadow Warriors. Greshane and Leinad quickly drew their swords. Their horses bolted from the rush of the ambush, and the two knights fought desperately against impossible odds. They fought back-to-back and used the dense forest to their advantage.

Greshane made quick work of two of the vicious warriors, and Leinad dropped another. Greshane now faced two enemies and Leinad faced one.

The Shadow Warriors were aggressive and powerful, but Leinad was quick and accurate. He parried and countered an explosive combination, then followed with a crosscut that cut deep into his opponent's torso. The Shadow Warrior dropped to the ground at the same instant that Leinad heard Greshane gasp in pain. With no foe facing him, he turned and saw one of the two Shadow Warriors withdraw a shallow but deadly thrust from Greshane's chest. Greshane narrowly parried a slice from the other before Leinad could cover for him. Greshane winced in pain but recovered his stance enough to face the Shadow Warriors again.

"Leave, Leinad! More will be coming, and you must find Gabrik!" Greshane said.

"I will not leave you, Greshane!" Leinad said amidst the clashing of swords.

"You must! Go now while I still have the strength to fend them off!"

Behind their opponents, Leinad could see an entire army of Shadow Warriors approaching.

"I will not leave you!" Leinad said defiantly.

Greshane was beginning to falter, and Leinad knew that it was a matter seconds before the Shadow Warrior would finish him off.

Just a couple of paces to his left, Leinad saw Greshane fall to one knee with his sword held limply before him. His enemy raised his sword to bring down a final deathblow upon Greshane's head.

Leinad opened himself up to his own opponent, and the Shadow Warrior anxiously took the opportunity and executed a powerful overextended thrust. But Leinad anticipated the move and used the split-second advantage to spin himself full circle away from his opponent and toward Greshane's.

In a blinding and powerful motion, Leinad transferred the speed of his circling maneuver into his blade as it screamed toward the up-stretched body of Greshane's executioner. His razor-sharp blade cut clean through Greshane's enemy, who fell backward, one blow short of another victory.

Leinad carried the momentum of his sword into a vertical cut as he stepped toward his own opponent and delivered a deadly blow to the shocked Shadow Warrior.

Leinad knelt down to Greshane.

"You must leave, Leinad." Greshane struggled for another breath as he clutched his chest. "It is pointless for both of us to die. You do not understand what is at stake…please…"

The force of brutal Shadow Warriors was approaching quickly.

"To leave you would deny all that I believe as a Knight of the King. I will not leave you, Greshane!"

Greshane grabbed Leinad's shoulder. "You are truly…a man of the Code. Help me stand then, that we might face our enemy…together."

Greshane made a monumental effort to stand, and Leinad helped him to his feet. They raised their swords to meet the oncoming ferocious attack of the Shadow Warriors.

"The King—" Greshane began to shout, but he could not finish, for the pain overwhelmed him.

"The King reigns!" Leinad shouted with his sword raised high.

Leinad heard movement behind him. He turned, and the entire forest seemed to move toward them. A large number of the King's Silent Warriors emerged from the trees and approached Greshane and Leinad.

Greshane fell to one knee again, and Leinad steadied him there. They had unknowingly traveled right into the leading edge of the battle between two mighty forces.

Gabrik quickly came to Leinad and Greshane and put his hand on Greshane's shoulder. "Well done, Greshane."

He ordered two other knights to carry Greshane out of the battlefront and then turned to Leinad.

"They outnumber us two to one, and our reinforcements are nowhere in sight. I did not intend for you to be here during this. Retreat to the rear, for it was not meant for you to fight these brutes, Leinad," Gabrik said, readying himself for the imminent fight.

Leinad raised his sword. "I hid from them once. I will not hide again!"

Gabrik smiled at the man he once knew as a boy. It was the only time Leinad had ever seen Gabrik smile.

"Leinad, you are highly favored by the King and by His warriors." Gabrik's smile turned to serious resolve.

"It is a good day to serve the King," Leinad said and stood beside Gabrik to face the wicked and overwhelming force that came at them.

An eerie battle cry precipitated the thunderous clash of

steel. Leinad was caught up in the secret world of battling giants—a world most of the kingdom was unaware of. He fought well. The King's training saved him and enabled him to survive and be victorious in each encounter.

But despite the gallant efforts of the Silent Warriors, the Shadow Warriors were too numerous. Gabrik stayed beside Leinad and fought courageously, But a surge of fresh Shadow Warriors renewed their attack, and the Silent Warriors stood on the edge of defeat.

Gabrik finished his immediate fight with a quick slice that ended the life of his opponent.

"Leinad, fall back. Lucius is leading this wave of warriors. It is time to retreat!"

Behind the line of Shadow Warriors, a man rode confidently and calmly up to the battlefront. He dismounted and advanced toward Gabrik and Leinad. He came with the confidence of a dragon. His manner left no question as to his identity. Leinad recognized him from that day many years ago in the forest. Anger began to burn within his blood as he remembered Lucius's cold-blooded murder of his father.

Gabrik grabbed Leinad's shoulder. "He comes for you and for me, Leinad, but neither of us can defeat him. To die seeking revenge is not noble. I must face him so you can take the promise to the people of Chessington."

Leinad quelled his anger and looked at Gabrik with questioning eyes.

"Gabrik!" The sharp voice of the Dark Knight cut through the sounds of battle like a sword itself. "You are finished, and the future of Arrethtrae is mine. You should have joined me across the sea when you had the opportunity. Instead you will die by my sword this very day!" Lucius spoke with an arrogance that matched his skill.

Gabrik prepared to face Lucius, and Leinad readied himself as well. For the first time since he'd known Gabrik, Leinad sensed deep apprehension in his lifelong secret companion. *The sword of Lucius must be deadly indeed,* Leinad thought.

"Step aside, men," came a voice from behind them.

Gabrik and Leinad turned to see a line of reinforcements join forces with the Silent Warriors. A powerful warrior Leinad had never seen before led them. His chest and arms were massive, and there was no hesitation in his approach.

"Micalem!" Gabrik said. "You have arrived."

Gabrik and Leinad stepped aside to allow Micalem access to the Dark Knight. He took a stance that evoked power and speed. He turned his head slightly toward Gabrik.

"I believe you have a mission to accomplish," he said and then refocused on Lucius.

Gabrik and Leinad instinctively backed away.

"Well, Micalem…I guess this is your day to die as well!" Lucius said.

"Your days are numbered, Lucius. Despite your arrogance, by the power of the King and the Prince, your future will be your ever-present fear!"

Micalem spoke the words with such assuredness that Lucius's only reply was a wrathful sword.

The two swords flew so powerfully and so swiftly that even Leinad was amazed. He had never witnessed the clash of such mastery before. It was a sight to behold, but Gabrik pulled him into retreat.

The refreshed Silent Warriors assumed the battle, and it raged on. Gabrik took Leinad to the small clearing where their horses were tied. Leinad only now felt the exhaustion of the battle settle upon him. Gabrik offered him water, and they both drank heavily.

A rider broke through the tree line from the west. "Sir Gabrik!" the rider called as he halted his steed just before them.

"Yes, Keef, what is your report?" Gabrik asked.

"I have just returned from Wolf Ridge. Last night Lucius dispatched the Arrethtraen force under Zane's command to the south. I fear they are headed toward Chessington. I would have reported sooner, but Lucius positioned his forces between us, and it took me until now to evade them."

Gabrik became solemn in momentary thought.

"I must leave for Chessington at once," Leinad said.

Leinad's brief encounter with Zane as a sixteen-year-old was enough for him to understand how wicked his estranged brother had become. It was hard for Leinad to think of Zane as a brother at all, for he was the epitome of all that Leinad strove to defeat.

"Yes," Gabrik said. "Unfortunately our forces will be unable to assist you until we can defeat Lucius here."

"I understand, Gabrik. The Noble Knights are ready. We will defend Chessington to the end."

"Keef, you will ride with Leinad as far as the river. Verify that Zane and his army are headed for Chessington, and report back as quickly as possible."

"Yes, sir. Give me a moment to find a fresh horse," he said to Leinad and left.

"Gabrik, Greshane said that this battle between the Shadow Warriors and us is to prevent the foretelling," Leinad said. "What is the foretelling, and why are the Shadow Warriors so concerned?"

"The foretelling is what will bring hope to Chessington and to all of Arrethtrae," Gabrik replied. "The King commissioned me to bring the foretelling to you, and were it not for Micalem, it wouldn't have happened." Gabrik took a deep breath and paused. "Leinad, the battle we are fighting here, and the battle the Noble Knights will fight in Chessington, is all about this."

Gabrik withdrew an item wrapped in cloth from his saddle and faced Leinad.

"This is the promise your father spoke of just before he died," Gabrik said reverently as he held the item before him. "Delivering it to you is the most important mission *I* will ever have. Delivering it to the people of Chessington will be the most important mission *you* will ever have."

Leinad held out his hands, and Gabrik laid the item in his open palms. He then opened the cloth to reveal the most beautiful sword Leinad had ever seen. Leinad gazed at the sword in astonishment. He slowly looked up at Gabrik in wonder.

"I have seen this magnificent sword once before, Gabrik. The man that carried it was fearless and noble. What does this mean?"

Gabrik stared into Leinad's eyes. "It is the promise, Leinad."

A FUTURE HOPE

 Leinad and Keef rode at full gallop back toward Chessington. Leinad carried the burden of knowing that his beloved city and his people would soon be under attack by a fierce army led by his own brother, but he also carried the promise that offered them hope of a bright future.

At the river, the tracks of many horses in the muddy shoreline made it obvious that Zane was headed straight for Chessington. Keef bid Leinad farewell and turned his steed back toward the Northern Mountains.

Leinad's anxiety grew with each stride of his horse. Though he had faith in the Noble Knights and in Audric's ability to command them, he did not know how large or how strong Zane's army was. The promise he carried from the King would be worthless if there were no people left to give it to.

And of course there was Tess. She would be at the leading

edge of the battle. Though she was any man's equal as a sword fighter, Leinad felt an urgency to be near to protect her. He attributed this to his role as her mentor, but in the quiet places of his heart resided a stronger motivating force than this.

Leinad entered the Chessington Valley in the early afternoon of a dark and cloudy day. The air was wet with mist that collected on his face until the drops fell down his brow and cheeks. This day was the culmination of his duty to the King as a knight, though it did not feel like the grand event it should have. He was weary, worried, and worn. The anticipation of battle was dulled because of his fatigue, and he wondered if he was capable of focusing on the tremendous task before him.

In the distance lay the beloved city of Chessington. Tiny figures formed a dark mass in the plains north of the city. Leinad estimated that Zane's forces outnumbered the Noble Knights five to one. Like a protective wall, the Noble Knights were positioned between their enemy and Chessington.

Leinad did not want to risk losing the precious sword of promise he carried in the throes of battle, so he placed it in the hollow of a large fallen tree.

Leinad saw the charge of Zane's army and felt the rush of war surge within his blood. His weariness released its hold on him, and he pressed his steed all the harder toward the converging armies. Just before he reached the battle, his exhausted horse collapsed beneath him, and Leinad fell to the ground. He rolled, recovered, drew his sword, and ran the remaining distance to the fight.

He did not hold back as he penetrated the deadly lines of Zane's forces from behind. Victory today would require a miracle, for Zane and his warriors were not the trivial bands of thieves that had raided Chessington in times past. They were vicious, battle experienced men.

Leinad vanquished enemy after enemy as he made his way to where he thought Tess was fighting.

The darkness of the day accentuated the darkness of the battle. There was no glory in the fighting—that would come later, when the swords were still and the spilled blood had disappeared into the soil. Leinad was not a warrior at heart, but he knew that war was the necessary evil to fight evil itself. He looked for the pasture of peace that lay beyond the trench of war.

The sound of a thousand clashing swords filled the air. The Noble Knights fought gallantly against these warriors who served Zane and ultimately the Dark Knight.

Leinad saw Audric and Tess immersed in the most intense part of the fight. He continued to work his way toward them until he came across one foe that would not fall.

Though Leinad had seen Zane only once before, the scar on his face left no doubt that the man he faced was his brother. Zane was an excellent swordsman, and his blows were powerful. Leinad remembered their encounter years ago in the forest north of his farm on the tragic day his father died. Zane's skill had improved significantly since then, or the rush of battle had heightened his performance, for Leinad found it difficult to capitalize on any weaknesses. Zane aggressively advanced on Leinad, but his sword met the guard of Leinad's mastery.

Zane paused. "Your fight feels familiar to me," he said.

Leinad glared at Zane in disgust. "Why do you serve the Dark Knight when you know the extent of his evil?"

Zane appeared surprised at the question. "Why does a man who is about to die ask such a foolish question?" Zane replied and attacked with a combination of cuts and slices.

"Because you were taught to love truth, honor, and justice...to be loyal to the King!" Leinad said with emotion.

"Those words are made of the fluff of clouds by the fools who chase them. The Dark Knight will rule Arrethtrae one day, and I will rule with him."

"He who serves the Dark Knight is a fool already," Leinad said.

Those words sparked a furious attack from Zane. Leinad defended each attack and countered with a powerful combination that put Zane in retreat.

The battle continued to rage about them, and Leinad was forced to disengage Zane and fight another. The relentless, brutal aggressors were overcoming the defenders of Chessington, and Leinad knew that his only hope to save the city lay in Zane. He faced two other warriors before he and Zane once again faced each other.

"Who are you?" Zane asked.

"I am who you should be—the son of Peyton, loyal Knight of the King!" Leinad could not deny the desire for his brother to turn from his evil ways and become a servant of the King.

Zane's sword nearly froze as he eyed Leinad with a look of astonishment. "You are the boy in the forest...the one who..." Zane's left hand slowly covered his right side where Leinad's sword had wounded him years ago. He scowled at Leinad. "Father was a fool. I led the Dark Knight to his home, and I took pleasure in killing one of his sons. Now I will kill another!"

Zane's confession and his lack of remorse released in Leinad a flood of righteous anger that no sword in Arrethtrae could defend. Leinad's sword flew like a falcon diving on its prey. His fury pounded upon Zane's defending sword like never before. The wicked, battle experienced warrior was in full retreat.

Leinad's continual onslaught of powerful and precise blows was too much for Zane. He stumbled over a body and fell to the ground. One of Zane's warriors turned on Leinad to save his leader, but with two quick cuts, the man lay dead on the ground beside Zane. Leinad held his sword at Zane's throat.

"Call for retreat, or your words of impertinence will be the last you ever speak!" Leinad said.

Zane glared back at Leinad, and his apparent hatred seemed to grow even deeper, but finally he nodded.

"Swear it!" Leinad shouted.

"I swear it," Zane said in a low, gruff voice.

Leinad let Zane rise but kept him at the tip of his sword until retreat was called and the dark forces of Zane's army were a good distance up the valley. One of Zane's men brought a horse for him to ride and waited twenty paces away.

By now Tess had joined Leinad at his side. He was relieved to see that she was unharmed.

"Is Audric all right?" he asked.

"Yes, he is attending to the men."

Zane stood still and silent.

"You may go," Leinad said to Zane, and he let the tip of his sword fall.

Zane eyed Leinad a moment longer. "I will destroy you, brother. One day, I will destroy you!"

Leinad looked on Zane and pity joined his anger. "You have already destroyed yourself, Zane."

Zane clenched his jaw and walked to his waiting horse. He mounted and pulled on the reins of the horse to face northward.

Leinad turned to face Tess. He breathed deeply and let the sight of his faithful friend begin to assuage his anger.

Tess looked at Leinad questioningly. "Brother?" she asked as she glanced toward the departing man.

Her eyes widened, and Leinad turned his head to see the cause of Tess's concern. He felt the push of her body as she threw herself against him and heard her gasp as they fell to the ground. He grabbed her to soften the impact and felt the handle of a knife protruding from her side.

"Tess!" he screamed.

Zane and the warrior with him bolted toward the rest of his army.

Tess closed her eyes, trying to bear the excruciating pain. Leinad laid her on the ground and screamed for Audric.

"Hold on, Tess!"

In one quick motion, Leinad pulled the knife from her side, and she screamed from the pain. He tried to bandage her wound the best he could, but the blood came too quickly. Near panic swept over him as the futility of his efforts bore down on him.

Leinad cradled Tess in his arms. The wound was deep, perhaps fatal. All of the emotions he had tried to bury over the past years surfaced in an unstoppable flood. His feelings for Tess had grown with each moment he spent with her. Sometimes it was subtle; sometimes it was obvious. All of the time he had spent denying the inevitable he now regretted. Tears welled up in his eyes, and he wished he could defy reality and recapture his time with her.

"Tess," he whispered. It was a name he had spoken a thousand times, but now it was so much more than the name of a fellow warrior.

Tess grimaced a gentle smile. She lifted her hand and touched his cheek. Her patient waiting was over. She could see that in his face.

She gathered strength to speak. "You…have been…and always will be…my hero."

Leinad wanted to take her place. If only he had kept his eyes on Zane until he had ridden away.

Leinad covered her hand with his own and pressed it tight against his cheek, then brought her hand to his lips, closed his eyes, and kissed her fingers. Two teardrops spilled from his eyes. He drew her closer and gazed into her eyes as he had never dared to before.

Her eyes returned his affection, and only now did he realize that her feelings for him had always been waiting…waiting for him to welcome them. What a fool he had been.

"I love you, Tess!" Impossible words yesterday now seemed so easy to say.

"I love you, Leinad!"

It was a union of two companion hearts. The walls of self-protection were down. Tess coughed and grimaced at the pain it brought, but the contented smile of a homecoming came to rest in its place. Leinad anguished over the possibility of losing his newly discovered love so quickly.

Audric knelt beside Leinad and placed a compassionate hand on his shoulder. The hushed silence of the Noble Knights was broken only by the distant sound of a galloping horse.

"Rider approaching," came the words from an anonymous voice. Leinad didn't care. These few moments with Tess were too precious.

The rider and his beast rushed near to Leinad and halted in a wash of wind. Gabrik dismounted before his steed had completely stopped. He ran to Leinad and Tess and knelt beside them. His stern, penetrating eyes were accompanied by a countenance of sorrow.

Leinad silently questioned Gabrik, who did not respond but immediately began to work on Tess's wound. The sweet odor of the same salve Gabrik had applied to the fatal wound of Leinad's father triggered the painful memories of many years ago.

"How effective is the Life Spice on such a wound?" Leinad asked.

Gabrik bandaged Tess's side, but the blood continued to soak through. "The wound is fresh, and the salve may save her life, but only temporarily. One can fully recover from a wound this deep only if the entire body absorbs the Life Spice."

A sliver of hope broke through the deep sorrow in Leinad's heart. "How is this...absorption accomplished?" he asked.

Tess moaned and Leinad grabbed her hand. She squeezed his hand to help bear the pain.

"Hang on, Tess!" Leinad said.

Her eyes rolled back and she closed them. Unconsciousness was near.

Leinad looked in earnest at Gabrik. "How?"

Gabrik was slow to answer. "She must be taken to a place where the food, the water, and even the air contain the Spice."

"Where is such a place?"

Gabrik made Tess drink from his water flask. Leinad grabbed Gabrik's massive arm and looked straight into his eyes.

Gabrik spoke quietly. "It is across the Great Sea."

One of the Noble Knights pointed to the north. "Sir Audric—look!"

Zane's army was fast approaching to finish the battle and take Chessington. The Noble Knights were weary and knew they could not withstand this evil army a second time.

"Ready yourselves, men!" Audric cried.

A line of gallant men, both wounded and whole, rose up to give their all in defense of their city and their people.

Leinad could not leave Tess, though he knew he must join his fellow knights in this final battle.

Gabrik finished a second wrap on the blood-soaked bandage and handed Leinad his flask.

"Keep her drinking the water," he said and rose from his work.

Leinad held Tess closely. She grimaced, and his sorrow turned to anger against his brother. It swelled within him, and his hand found the hilt of his sword. Zane deserved to die, and nothing would stop Leinad from executing the judgment he deserved. Leinad regretted the mercy he had granted his evil brother, for it might cause the death of his faithful friend—his love.

"Zane will die for this offense!" he said fiercely. He began to lay Tess on the ground, but she found the strength to grab his arm. She looked gently into his eyes. "No more killing, Leinad," she said softly.

Leinad touched her cheek, and she smiled. He marveled at her beauty both inside and out. Then unconsciousness overcame her.

He looked up and saw the dark army descending upon the Noble Knight remnant. The rumble of horses' hooves beat upon the ground, and the earth shook beneath them.

"If only I could stop it, I would, Sunshine," he said sadly.

Just then Leinad heard the blast of a trumpet. Gabrik stood before the Noble Knights with his sword in one hand and a golden trumpet in the other. The valley was filled with the brilliant pitch of the lone horn.

From beyond both sides of the near horizons, a force of mounted men began to appear until there was no gap in the majestic line of Silent Warriors that framed the valley. They drew their swords and held them aloft.

Zane's army slowed its advance to a stop as the men

gazed in fearful dread at the massive force that encompassed them from above. An eerie silence lasted for a moment and then was broken by the rumble of horses' hooves as the army fled north once again, this time to save their lives.

The Noble Knights cheered, and the people of Chessington rejoiced to see their enemies disappear from their valley.

Leinad's rejoicing was constrained by the anguish in his heart. Tess's breathing was shallow and irregular. Gabrik returned to Leinad and knelt beside him.

"I will take her across the sea," Leinad said, denying what he knew was not possible.

"I'm sorry, Leinad. You know it is not allowed," Gabrik said. "She may go, but she cannot return. I know it is hard for you, but at least she will live."

Leinad was torn inside, but there was no decision for him to make. She might live for a time in Arrethtrae, but eventually she would die. He could not risk Tess's life for a few years of companionship.

Leinad leaned close to his newfound love and kissed her forehead. "I love you, Tess," he whispered.

Tess opened her eyes. "I would rather die than live apart from you, Leinad." Though her voice was weak, the sparkle in her eyes reflected the inner strength Leinad had come to rely upon year after year. "I will not go."

"But if you remain here, you might die, Tess," Leinad argued against his warring heart.

"I…" she found another breath of air "…will not go!"

Leinad gazed into her eyes and smiled. "I've never

known a woman like you, Tess." He leaned closer and
held her tightly.

THE SILENT WARRIORS RETURNED to the realm of secrecy
from which they had come, and Tess was safely transported
back to Chessington. Leinad left her side only long enough
to say good-bye to Gabrik, his lifelong mentor, protector,
and friend, who had lingered to say farewell until after Tess
had been cared for.

"You were victorious over the Shadow Warriors then?"
Leinad asked Gabrik.

"Yes."

"Did Micalem defeat the Dark Knight?"

"He was deterred, but he will return, Leinad. One day
he will return. You must prepare the people, for he wants
to rule Arrethtrae, and Chessington stands in his way."

Leinad nodded, but at the moment such thoughts were
overwhelming.

"When will I see you again, Gabrik?" Leinad asked.

"Maybe tomorrow...maybe never. Only the King
knows, my friend."

Leinad knew by his tone that their missions were on
different paths now.

"Thank you, Gabrik," Leinad said. "Thank you for
everything."

Gabrik nodded, and the two men embraced.

Gabrik mounted his steed and saluted Leinad.
"Remember the promise, my friend. Remember and
believe."

Leinad saluted back, and Gabrik rode out of Chessington.

Leinad returned to Tess. Audric soon came, and Leinad sent him north to retrieve the sword of promise from the fallen tree. Then he waited…waited for his Tess to recover. For the promise was for people who had a heart like hers—a heart that was faithful to the Code and to the King.

FIVE DAYS LATER, TESS WAS strong enough to sit up, and the color in her cheeks was pink again. Leinad held her hand and smiled. On the battlefield, their lifelong relationship had changed in a moment, and now a river of newly expressed love flowed between them.

"Tell me, did you find the vision you've been searching for?" Tess asked. "Did you find the key to the kingdom?"

"Yes, Sunshine, I did." Leinad reached for the majestic sword still wrapped in its cloth and held it before her. "It is a promise for the people…for all of us."

Tess's eyes gleamed, and she lifted her hand to touch Leinad's cheek. "Deliver the promise, Leinad."

THE SQUARE OF THE CITY WAS filled with all the people of Chessington. The midafternoon air was cool, but the bright sun was unhampered by a cloudless sky, and it warmed the skin. Beside the oak tree in the center of the square, Leinad sat tall upon his powerful horse so all could see him. Audric, Tess, and all the Noble Knights were by his side.

"Noble people of Chessington, today is the day of hope

for us all—hope for a future kingdom that will surpass the glory of the days of Quinn. My father saw the dawn of the kingdom of Arrethtrae, but we stand in a kingdom that is on the precipice of true greatness. In the Red Canyon, the King gave us the Code to live by, and it was our guide and our light through many dark days. Today He gives us the key to that future great kingdom. It is…" Leinad withdrew the majestic sword and held it high for all to see, "…the sword of promise."

An exclamation of awe swept through the people, for they had never seen a sword of such magnificence. The golden hilt supported the gleaming steel of the blade as the sun reflected off its edge.

"What is the promise?" asked a young man in the crowd.

"It is the promise that one who is worthy will someday take up this sword and be our king. He will deliver us from the Dark Knight and his evil Shadow Warriors. The one who is worthy will save us! The one who is worthy is the coming Prince!"

A cheer rose up, and all the people rejoiced at the promise of the coming Prince. They celebrated with a feast to remember their past and to embrace their future. For a time, they forgot their fear and their sorrow, and the promise of the Prince gave them the hope of a future for which they longed.

OF BATTLE
AND OF PEACE

Leinad and Tess were true Knights of the King, and I, Cedric of Chessington, am honored to be part of their chronicle. My story begins where their story ends. Although many of the people eventually lost hope and forgot the promise of the coming Prince, Leinad and Tess stayed true and faithful. They married and enjoyed many joyful years together. When Tess eventually grew faint and the Silent Warriors carried her across the Great Sea, Leinad persevered in his mission into old age. He strove to keep the promise and the Code alive, but even the Noble Knights lost sight of the true meaning of the Code and forgot the promise.

Though Leinad was saddened by the apathy of the people, his words found a welcome home in the heart of a young boy. That is where his life touched mine and changed me forever. My story I will gladly tell you…but it must be another time, for now it is time to prepare for battle.

Dawn is breaking in the kingdom before us. It is a kingdom that is ravaged by the greedy whims of the evil one. A kingdom once bold and beautiful is now oppressed under bondage. But soon we will deliver her, for the Deliverer is here. Those who have found the faith and remain true to the Prince will be rewarded. All others will be judged and condemned.

If you knew the Prince as I do, you would know as I do in my heart that the outcome of our battle is sure. I cannot deny the skipped beat of my heart within my chest, but it is not for fear…it is for anticipation. Where will this journey with the Prince end? What grand adventure lies beyond this battle? I do not know, but one thing I do know: I will stay by His side! None other is worthy of such devotion, only the Prince.

He is the majestic one that will lead us. There is no hesitation in His movements or question in His eyes. He will lead us to a new beginning. The new kingdom's dawn will start today. It will be a dawn to usher in an age of peace. But peace must be bought, and this battle will be the price.

There is a mighty and evil force before us, but I am not afraid. I am on the side of the Prince.

DISCUSSION QUESTIONS

To further facilitate the understanding of the biblical allegory of this series, a few discussion questions and answers are provided below.

CHAPTER 1

1. Who does Leinad represent in this chapter?

2. Throughout the next couple chapters there is an obvious change in Leinad's attitude. Although in all his previous fights he fought in the name of the King, Leinad fought trusting in his own ability. Now Leinad trusts completely in the King, and Leinad experiences sword fighting success as he never has before. Interestingly enough, Leinad also isn't afraid anymore. Second Timothy 1:7 says, "For God has not given us a spirit of fear, but of power and of love and of a sound mind." Have you ever faced a daunting task but found it wasn't scary because of your trust in God?

CHAPTER 2

1. What do you think the Life Spice symbolizes?

2. Fairos swears by his sword that he won't ever free the slaves, and Leinad responds that Fairos swears in vain. What does the Bible say about swearing an oath?

CHAPTER 3

1. What is the event portrayed in this chapter?

2. The slaves worry that Fairos will increase their torment if Leinad wins the duel once again. Have you ever felt persecuted for making a stand? What were the circumstances?

CHAPTER 4

1. The people of Chessington are pursued by Fairos and his mounted army. Leinad discovers a small passageway into the canyon, and the people flee through it. When Fairos and his army try to travel through, however, an earthquake causes the passageway to collapse on the whole army, killing them. What biblical event does this portray?

2. Who do you think the massive warriors are?

3. The people escape from Fairos and his army, and they begin to praise Leinad for saving them. However, Leinad responds that their escape was brought about by the King; Leinad only followed the King's directions. This kind of behavior pleases the King; it also pleases God. Have you ever seen someone take credit for something they didn't do? Have you been tempted to accept credit for something God has done?

CHAPTER 5

1. Leinad and Tess climb the canyon walls to be with the King. Who do they represent here? Can you find the passage in Scripture for this scene?

2. What do the Articles of the Code represent?

CHAPTER 6

1. In this chapter Leinad represents a new biblical character. Who is he now?

2. We hear about the Knights of Chessington for the first time. Who do you think they represent?

3. Leinad asks Quinn if Moradiah, Quinn's betrothed, has a "heart for the King." Leinad understood the significance of 2 Corinthians 6:14. Look up that verse.

DISCUSSION QUESTIONS

Why do you think it is so important?

4. Toward the end of this chapter, Leinad's biblical representation changes again. Who does he represent now? Who does Lady Moradiah represent?

5. Quinn and Lady Moradiah begin their reign over Arrethtrae in "self-glorification." Quinn didn't start out so prideful; his relationship with Moradiah slowly distracted him from having an attitude the King would approve of. Have you ever found yourself saying things or doing things because your friends influenced you?

CHAPTER 7

1. Lady Moradiah is charismatic, and when she speaks, her words flow "like sweet honey from the comb." Often the people who speak the sweetest words have bitter lies they're trying to hide. Have you ever heard something that sounded good, but you knew it was a lie?

2. The first significant event in this chapter is when Leinad single-handedly defeats all of Lady Moradiah's knights. What biblical event does this represent?

3. Soon the people of Chessington resent Leinad's presence. Every time they see him they are reminded of their apathy toward following the King and the Code. Have you ever felt like other people were annoyed with you because of your faith?

4. When Leinad tries to warn the people and he is ridiculed, his biblical representation changes again. Who does he represent now?

5. Leinad receives a message from the King to allow Kergon and the Kessons to overtake Chessington, but

Quinn's pride causes him to refuse to obey the King's wishes. Because of Quinn's refusal to listen to the King, the City of Chessington is decimated. What biblical event does this portray?

CHAPTER 8

1. Who does Leinad represent in this chapter?

CHAPTER 9

1. Leinad, Tess, and Audric refuse to kneel and swear allegiance to Kergon. What biblical event does this portray?

2. Who do Tess and Audric represent in this chapter?

3. Leinad, Tess, and Audric make a stand against Kergon. They refuse to swear allegiance to someone other than the King, even though they know they will die for their convictions. Have you ever made a stand when the consequences seemed like they would be more than you could bear?

4. A stranger rides out from the lair of the dragamoths and aids Leinad, Tess, and Audric in their struggle against the beasts. What two biblical events does this portray?

5. Who do you think the "man from a distant land" is in the Kingdom Series? Who do you think he represents?

6. Tess says, "I am afraid, Audric, but I am not a coward." Courage isn't the absence of fear; it's what you do in spite of fear. Have you ever done something for God even though you were scared at the time?

CHAPTER 10

1. Leinad begins to wonder if his purpose is to guide the people of Chessington from disaster to peace over and

over again. Then Leinad realizes that the time of captivity in Daydelon is almost over for the people of Chessington. His reflection is interrupted by a Silent Warrior's message from the King: Kergon will be destroyed and his rule over the people of Chessington will end, so they can return to their beloved city. What do the events in this chapter represent biblically?

2. Leinad tells the people of Chessington not to despair, because the King of Arrethtrae is "with us...we are His people. One day He will bring peace to Arrethtrae. There will be no more slavery, no more fighting, no more thirsting, and no more hunger." What is this a foreshadowing of? What does this represent biblically?

3. Leinad tells the people of Chessington that the "King did not leave us; we left the King." God promised that He will "never leave you nor forsake you" (Hebrews 13:5b). Have you ever left God's will, but found Him waiting for you to return to Him? Find more verses in the Bible regarding God's promise to never leave us.

CHAPTER 11

1. In this chapter, who does Leinad represent?

2. Who do the Noble Knights represent?

3. Leinad refuses to leave Greshane even though it means Leinad may die at the hands of Shadow Warriors. Greshane says, "You are truly...a man of the Code." Greshane is referring to the fifth Article of the Code: "Never abandon a fellow knight in battle or in peril." Leinad shows what he truly believes by staying with Greshane. Remember that actions speak louder than words. Have you ever had an opportunity to be a witness by your actions?

4. Gabrik is delayed in giving Leinad the foretelling because the Dark Knight and his Shadow Warriors keep him preoccupied in battle. (Look up Daniel 10:10–14 and 10:20–21.) What does it represent biblically?

5. What is the foretelling?

CHAPTER 12

1. Leinad experiences righteous anger when he realizes that his brother Zane feels no remorse or sorrow for his wickedness. There is a passage in the Bible regarding righteous anger. Find that verse.

2. Leinad gives the people the "promise." Find other Old Testament passages that give the Jews and the whole world the promise that a Savior was to come to earth and save us.

3. The promise of the coming Prince was fulfilled when Jesus was born. His mission on earth was to teach us about God and to die on the cross for our sins. The Bible tells us that anyone who believes in Jesus and that God raised Him from the dead will be saved. John 3:16 says, "For God so loved the world that He gave His only begotten Son, that whoever believes in Him should not perish but have everlasting life." Have you ever put your faith and trust in Jesus?

ANSWERS TO
DISCUSSION QUESTIONS

CHAPTER 1

1. Moses.

2. Answer based on personal experience.

CHAPTER 2

1. The Life Spice represents the "Spirit of life" or the "breath of life" described in Revelation 11:11. It also represents the immortality that we receive as believers in Jesus after the resurrection.

2. The Bible says that we are held accountable for every word we speak. Therefore, we should be very careful as it says in James 5:12: "But above all, my brethren, do not swear, either by heaven or by earth or with any other oath. But let your 'Yes' be 'Yes,' and your 'No,' 'No,' lest you fall into judgment."

CHAPTER 3

1. The last plague (death of the firstborn) as written in Exodus 12:29.

2. Answer based on personal experience.

CHAPTER 4

1. The children of Israel fleeing through the Red Sea.

2. Silent Warriors, or angels.

3. Answer based on personal experience.

CHAPTER 5

1. Leinad represents Moses, and Tess represents Joshua (see Exodus 32).

2. The Ten Commandments.

CHAPTER 6

1. Samuel.

2. The religious leaders of the Jews and, more specifically, the priests (Levites).

3. The Bible warns us to not be "unequally yoked together with unbelievers." If we are, our service to the Lord can be hindered, and we will probably face many additional challenges in life.

4. Leinad represents Elijah, and Moradiah represents Jezebel.

5. Answer based on personal experience.

CHAPTER 7

1. Answer based on personal experience.

2. Elijah and the prophets of Baal offering sacrifices to their gods.

3. Answer based on personal experience.

4. Jeremiah.

5. The fall of Jerusalem as prophesied in Jeremiah 27.

CHAPTER 8

1. Daniel.

CHAPTER 9

1. Three faithful servants of God refusing to bow before King Nebuchadnezzar, as written in Daniel 3:8–18.

2. Shadrach, Meshach, and Abednego.

3. Answer based on personal experience.

4. This event has dual symbolism to show Daniel in the lion's den and the fiery furnace of King Nebuchadnezzar.

5. He is the King's son, the Prince. Biblically, He is the preincarnate Christ.

6. Answer based on personal experience.

CHAPTER 10

1. Daniel's realization that the Israelites' time of captivity is almost over (Jeremiah 29:10 and Daniel 9:2), the fall of Babylon, and the return of the Jews to Israel.

2. This foreshadows when the King and the Prince establish peace in the new Arrethtrae. This represents Christ's return and the peace He will establish on earth when He reigns.

3. Answer based on personal experience.

CHAPTER 11

1. Nehemiah (read Nehemiah 2:5).

2. The religious leaders who eventually become the Pharisees.

3. Answer based on personal experience.

4. The spiritual battle between the angels and the demons. The event specifically represents the demons' desperate attempt to keep the angel of God from delivering messianic prophecies to Daniel.

5. The message that the Prince is coming to save the kingdom. In this scene, it directly symbolizes the incredible prophecy given to Daniel (Daniel 9:20–27).

CHAPTER 12

1. Ephesians 4:26.

2. Isaiah 7:14; 53:1–12; Jeremiah 31:31–34; Micah 5:2; Zechariah 9:9.

3. Answer based on personal experience.

Discovery

Written for Kingdom's Hope

Music by Emily Elizabeth Black
Lyrics by Chuck Black
Edited by Brittney Dyanne Black

Hope... gives us a light in the dark

Hope... breaks thru the chains and brings joy to the heart.

Who... heralds His Word to the end? He... seeks for the

meek and the hum-ble to send.

King of Kings and Lord of Lords gives hope to all who fol- low. Come and join the King and the Prince, take up the sword of Life. Tar- ry not, be brave & strong, put on the heart of cour- age. Take His Word to all in the land and break the bonds of strife.

AUTHOR'S COMMENTARY

The prophets of the Old Testament were men of great faith and conviction. Chastised, beaten, and even killed for the words of truth God gave them to speak to the people, they courageously fulfilled their mission in spite of the inevitable fear they must have felt. In many instances, God intervened to protect them and, more importantly, to reaffirm the truth and authenticity of their message. It is because of the valor of these men that we have the prophecies and unapologetic truth of the Old Testament today.

Through the fulfillment of these prophecies, the incredible truth of God's Word becomes evident and builds faith. At times God's message to the people was one of blessing and prosperity. At other times it was a message of discipline and punishment because of the sinful hearts of the people.

The prophets often felt abandoned by God's people, but the Lord always preserved a faithful remnant. These were the men and women who stayed true to God despite the lure of the world. Their hearts were every bit as courageous and bold as those of the prophets. Through them, God also revealed His love, faithfulness, and compassion. Together, the *faithful* and the *prophets* brought the resounding message of hope to the world—the message of a redeemer—to the humble and to the meek.

Kingdom's Hope, the second book in the Kingdom Series, has told the story of these chosen few through allegory. The following paragraphs reveal some of the analogy between the adventures of Leinad and Tess and the true story of the prophets and people of the Old Testament.

Once again, as in *Kingdom's Dawn,* Cedric tells the story of his mentor, Leinad. In *Kingdom's Edge,* book three, Cedric will be the central character, but *Kingdom's Dawn* and *Kingdom's Hope* focus on Leinad, who represents characters and prophets from the Old Testament. With this understanding, one can see Moses, Elijah, Jeremiah, Daniel, Nehemiah, Malachi, and others all represented at various times in the character of Leinad.

Tess and Audric represent the faithful remnant that stayed true to the Lord and did not abandon the prophets even when the rest of the nation turned its back on them. Some literary freedom was used to develop the romance between Tess and Leinad. However, one could speculate that there was a special understanding and relationship between the faithful and the prophets. Tess and Audric represent such biblical characters as Joshua, Caleb, Debra, Ruth, Jabez, and Jonathan.

Quinn represents the kings, both good and bad, of Israel and Judah. As a whole, their commitment to the Lord was as wavering as that of the people and in some cases much worse.

The Silent Warriors represent God's holy angels. Conversely, the Dark Knight and the Shadow Warriors represent Satan and the fallen angels. Zane represents the unrepentant mass of mankind that begins with Cain and carries through to the evil people at the time of Noah's flood and beyond. The redemption of Zane is not an impossibility, for God desires that none should perish: "that whoever believes in Him should not perish but have eternal life" (John 3:15).

The sword in all of the Kingdom Series novels represents the Word of God. The challenge in *Kingdom's Dawn* and *Kingdom's Hope* was differentiating between the real swords used in the Old Testament battles and the "Word of God" sword used by the prophets to reveal God's will to the people. Extreme care was taken to create allegorical content centered on the sword that directly symbolized God's Word through the prophets.

Many significant biblical events are portrayed, such as the release from captivity in Egypt, the wandering in the wilderness, the receiving of the Law, the glorious days of David, the Babylonian captivity, and the rebuilding of the city of Jerusalem. Many of these biblical events were prophesied. Probably one of the most dramatic prophecies ever given is the messianic prophecy given to Daniel (Daniel 9:22–27). This incredible prophecy of Jesus Christ's arrival, triumphal entry into Jerusalem, and eventual earthly reign is the substance for the climactic scene at the end of the book. It was through men like Daniel and his Holy Spirit inspired words that the people were given hope…hope of a Savior to come.

Kingdom's Hope concludes at the end of the Old Testament, where the prophets faded into the past and all waited for their prophecies to be fulfilled. Unfortunately, as time wore round the edges of expectation of the coming Messiah, those most qualified to recognize Him were blind and unaware that He was suddenly among them.

It is my earnest hope and prayer that all who read this novel will be inspired to search the Scriptures and recognize the one who is among us even now and call Him Lord. Our only hope is in Jesus Christ alone!

As it is written in the Prophets:
"Behold, I send My messenger before Your face,
Who will prepare Your way before You."
Mark 1:2